French Seduction

ALSO BY EUNICE LIPTON

Alias Olympia:
A Woman's Search for Manet's Notorious Model
and Her Own Desire

Looking into Degas:
Uneasy Images of Women and Modern Life

Picasso Criticism, 1901–1939:
The Making of an Artist-Hero

French Seduction

An American's Encounter with France,
Her Father, and the Holocaust

EUNICE LIPTON

CARROLL & GRAF PUBLISHERS
NEW YORK

FRENCH SEDUCTION
An American's Encounter with France, Her Father, and the Holocaust

Carroll & Graf Publishers
An Imprint of Avalon Publishing Group, Inc.
245 West 17th Street
11th Floor
New York, NY 10011

AVALON
publishing group incorporated

Library of Congress Cataloging-in-Publication Data is available.

ISBN-13: 978-0-78671-626-5
ISBN-10: 0-7867-1626-6

9 8 7 6 5 4 3 2 1

Interior design by Maria E. Torres

Printed in the United States of America
Distributed by Publishers Group West

French Seduction

For Kathy –
with great expectations
of shared books &
times in NY–or Paris.

5/15/07

Introduction

Love Story

My father whispers, "Darling, go to Paris. You'll be happy there, you'll see."

Of course, he's never been. My Pop's a dreamer and a fantasist. I know that from the start. As a little girl, I watch him in his candy store in the Bronx. I see him in the late afternoon at the end of the long white Formica counter, hunched over *Life* magazine. The sun slants in through the windows, the mint-green neon sign pulses "Luncheonette." In New York in the late 1940s, a candy store could also be a luncheonette. He says to me, pointing to a picture, "That's the Seine, Eunie." And he stares at it. "Pretty, isn't it?" I see nice-looking people holding hands, everyone happy. He turns the page to a photograph of an outdoor café, and tells me about Zola. "A great French writer," he says. "Of course, he knew a different Paris than these pictures. He knew poor people, hardworking people. Like us. Except they were goyim."

A few minutes later he closes the magazine, forgetting that I'm looking, too.

My father was born in Riga, Latvia, and left for America when he was fifteen. That's when his fantasies about France began. Kids in New York probably greeted his "I'm from Riga" with that famous American "Huh?" So he started saying he came from the Paris of the North. What I really believe, though, is that he was waiting for me to come along to listen to his dreams. A besotted daughter's fantasy, no doubt.

My dad's father, Max, took his sons out of Europe in the 1920s. Russians and Germans were grabbing Jewish boys off the streets and throwing them into their armies, and he was frightened. Then, too, there were the family letters from Russia about pogroms. Later, everyone said the decision to leave was the only thing my grandpa ever put his foot down about. It was a way of criticizing him, and it always bothered me. My grandmother, Anna, was the decisive one, they said. People turned my grandpa into a weak man, as if a strong man could never, would never, want to be with an opinionated woman like Grandma. I knew they were dead wrong.

My father worked for his parents in their specialty grocery store in Riga. His responsibility was the chocolates. He spoke Yiddish, Russian, some German. He went to school and played soccer. He learned about sex from the family's maids. When he was six, he had a withering experience that he never spoke about. It would be eighty years before he told me the story.

I'm sure that at fifteen my father—Louis, pronounced Louie—was a smiling, seductive boy and didn't want to leave home. But like two million other Jews from Eastern Europe, that's what he did. The family slid from the middle class into the working class when they left their lucrative business behind and used their savings for steamship tickets. Grandpa and his three sons—Phil, Dave, and my father—became house painters. There weren't going to be any maids in New York.

But there was going to be a lot of dancing. My Pop became a much sought-after partner, and soon he found my mother, who was also crazy for dancing. She was fifteen, he eighteen. He boxed, too, and competed in the Golden Gloves. And he made all-night drives to Miami—to pick up fruit, he said. In the 1930s and '40s he sailed to Batista's Cuba, a mobster's playground. Grandma worried about him. "He's too clever," she said appreciatively. When I'm a teenager, my father makes me uncomfortable by telling me stories about boys in Havana who sell their sisters as prostitutes to Americans.

My dad loved conversation and nice clothes and Paris, and I loved him. So when I am nineteen, I save my money and board a student ship to France. I write him postcards all summer long, every couple of days or so, sometimes more. I tell him how much I miss him. I report on the sights. "Dear Daddy, Try to imagine this Byzantine structure," I write him about Sacré Coeur in Montmartre, "amidst one of the poorest sections in

Paris. Very incongruous! Nancy and I came back to the hotel and had a small supper of oranges, bread, cheese, and wine. Delicious! I'm resting now, so I'm thinking of you. All my love. . . ."

My whole life, I will write to men I love this way, even if they live just across town, or, now, in the case of my husband working in his studio, just across the courtyard. I remember the smell of the postcards and paper on which I wrote my first boyfriend. I'm fifteen, and I tell him of *Jude the Obscure* and Thelonious Monk, the sun sliding into my room, the snow I imagine him surrounded by on his two weeks away from me with his college pals. The cards and letters end with "I love you." I am an enchantress. I weave my feelings and thoughts into words. The lines and curves of the letters wind around my beloved, pulling him to me. This is something I learned with my father.

That first charmed summer in France in 1960, in a room near the Boulevard St. Michel, I taste my first croissant. I am amazed at what they let you eat for breakfast. I'm used to squares, rectangles, ovals, and circles. White bread, rye bread, bagels, and Danish. But a layered crescent, golden, flaky, and fresh as the challah my grandma made on Fridays? This was cake for breakfast, and you weren't ruining your appetite, as your mother would say—you were satisfying it.

That same morning, I walk a few blocks along my Pop's Seine to Notre Dame. Churches aren't places Jewish kids go into. In Hurleyville, the town in the Catskills where my grandparents finally settle, there are two white churches, one Catholic, one Protestant. I never even want to walk on the same side of the road. I sneak a look at the colored glass in one of the doors and then avert my eyes, as if I could die for just looking. I avoid the crosses. My father hates churches. *"Anti-Semitin,"* he spits out.

But Notre Dame is one of the great sights of Paris. I can't not go in.

The slim, smiling saints gaze down from the doors. Aloof and sane, they are like the trees along the boulevard. Inside, drops of red, green, yellow, and blue stain the floor. I look up and find the astonishing glass of Notre Dame. The stories there tell of simple men and women ennobled by their experience of God. Febrile arches stretch to Gothic points, bundles of stone rods hug columns and pull them skyward. Notre Dame's central aisle soars like a missile to heaven. I feel secure here, and calm.

France, as something of my very own, begins in the sweet beauty of this church.

———

In my mid-twenties, I fall in love with Philippe, a boy who is half French and half Jewish. He is a sly, witty fellow with a long, high-cheekboned face, blue eyes, and shapely hands. His light brown hair slides forward to his forehead, and he has a little round swelling near the edge of his mouth that's an advertisement for languor. It's as if in the making of his face, the sculptor's hand slowed, and the matter she was working concentrated into this beautiful little spot, this punctuation mark that says "Hold on a minute, there's plenty of time."

Words and actions dally with Philippe. A smile hovers around his eyes as if his thoughts amuse him. Even after we live together for several years, in the late 1960s, and I know how unhappy he is, still I witness his pleasure at seeing the world anew each day. Poised for the next surprise, he bides his time. Sometimes it comes in a sentence of a Jorge Luis Borges story, or the discovery of a mislaid jar of candied chestnuts. Sometimes it's just the curve of a building.

Philippe loves conversation. The kitchen table in our New York apartment is like a dance floor where words dip and turn and sidle. He never patiently waits his turn to then launch into oration. He listens, delighted or perplexed, responding with appreciation or embellishment, or with a suggestion of something slightly different, something otherwise, with him, no one has to win. One night when a friend comes to dinner, the three of us look up at a reproduction of Henri Rousseau's *Carnival Evening* above the table. Each of us ruminates about the mysterious forest where masked revelers lose their way. Paintings, words, food get all mixed up. Meals are unspeakably satisfying.

When Philippe and I talk, time slows down. Over the years, this is what France comes to mean to me, too, this stretching-out of the moment, the savoring of words, ideas, the senses. This aimless unfurling reminds me of conversations with my father about people in books, and of spinning arm in arm with him on the ice in Central Park, hip to hip, shoulder to shoulder, inhaling each other's breath, the push and glide of our bodies, those meandering pleasures. People used to think we were a couple.

My dad was a champion listener: "Is that so?" "I didn't know that." "You really think so?" He could be spectacularly present as he looked right into your eyes, touched your hand. But he could also suddenly turn and vanish. Or he could churn like a tornado and smash you with his rage. You couldn't be too sure with him.

It's 1978 and it's the first time he visits me in Paris—the first time he's ever been to Paris. I find him a charming little room on the Left Bank, his perfect room, just like the one in his favorite opera, *La Bohème*. We climb the stairs. I open the door. He takes a quick look around and bellows, "A whore wouldn't stay here." He slams the door and charges out of the hotel, never even saying thank you to the proprietor. I so wanted to show him a Paris that would delight him and prick his fantasies, that would show him how much I love him. But he wants "modern," or, more precisely, something that shows how far he's come up in the world. And he behaves as if I am trying to kill him by having chosen this little room.

Loving people and insulting them freely comes naturally to my father. When I'm forty and marry for a second time, he remarks that Ken, my new husband, hasn't read enough literature, that he and his family are not as cultivated as the Liptons—that, in a word, they are uncouth Americans. He says this to Ken's face, smiling all the time, as if he's announcing a fact, and being magnanimous by telling the truth. Ken is shocked. He's just met my father. He changes the subject. But I don't. I suggest to my father that what he has said is not very nice. He roars at me that I don't know what a sick man he is. Which, by the way, he is not.

My father didn't like Philippe either, but for a different reason. "He's not very manly," he said.

———

Louis thought art was Christian. It was something he associated with churches. Yet I became an art historian. I was never able to convince him of the pleasures of seeing. I suppose it's not something you learn late in life. He preferred touch and sound. He hugged you, he kissed you, he talked to you. The story goes that he had lots of lovers. An aunt of mine told me this when I was eleven.

If my father was all touch and talk, sight becomes my special sense and, it turns out, my magic wand. I remember the day it made its appearance. I am four and living with my grandparents in the country. It's winter. Grandpa and I are returning from a sleigh ride to town. Grandma, despite the cold, is standing at the gate wearing only a housedress. She holds a copy of *Life* magazine. She pushes it toward Grandpa. *"Gib a kik*, Max," she says. Take a look. He does. Then he lets the magazine fall to the snow. I look down and see skinny people in striped pajamas. Grandma is crying. So is Grandpa. He drops my hand and hugs Grandma. They stand there weeping, ignoring me. Finally, Grandpa says to his wife, "Anna, Eunice was looking forward to a plate of your nice soup. Me too, darling."

We eat in silence except for the spoons clanging the china. I search the room for something to look at, a place to climb into. I find the blood-red geraniums on the windowsill throbbing against the snow. My eyes move to the left and stop on a framed picture of a sick girl who is stretched out on two chairs, her parents and a doctor nearby. The girl's red hair spreads sadly on a pillow. A rickety wooden table, some medicine and spoons, a kerosene lamp punctuate the darkness. I see the leaning doctor, the worried parents, the earthen colors.

I know the girl is going to die and that her parents will always miss her. Looking at this picture calms me. (Many years later, I learn that the girl is actually a boy.)

It is the first time that I remember looking hard at something. Probably I had done it before. The contrasts between the colors, lines, shapes, textures of the Bronx, where I lived with my parents, and the countryside around my grandparents' home must have been extreme. Surely I noticed, even without knowing it, the black-greens of pines, their thickly layered coffee-colored barks, the bleach-white snow and blue sky, the call to see, compared to the city's drab gray asphalt and mauve brick.

Looking at pictures will always be intertwined in my mind with the murder of Jews—those awful striped pajamas—and with my hunger for my grandparents' love and the knowledge that I might lose them forever, as I had during those momentary eternities when they ignored me while we stood in the snow and sat around the table. I learned that day how completely a person can be betrayed. I had conveniently forgotten that just a week earlier, my mother had pressed me into my grandfather's arms, shut the car door, and quite disappeared. Paintings will become a place for me to repress these feelings of betrayal and abandonment, these premonitions of death. But paintings also ferry me across them. They become my favorite companions.

I turn back to the table. My grandparents are still there. "Child," Grandma says, cupping my cheek with her hand, "wouldn't you like some more soup?"

I always say I fell into art history accidentally. It was an odd choice for a girl with my working-class, leftist family background. History would have made more sense, or literature. But a professor who was a medievalist and who came from Riga, like my father, suggested that I write a paper on some wall paintings in Siena, Italy, and that's how I became an art history major. Perhaps it was also a way of climbing out of the Bronx. Perhaps art was my Paris from the start. By the time I got to graduate school, I had left the Italians behind and chosen French art as my subject.

Once I became an art history professor, I began going to France every summer to do research. One of my projects takes me, in 1978, to Provence. I am curious about the famously warm friendship between Edgar Degas and a man named Evariste de Valernes who lived in the Vaucluse, in a town called Carpentras, north of Marseilles, east of Avignon. After doing a few weeks of research there, I decided to visit Monieux, where Valernes was born. It sits at the foot of Mont Ventoux, a sandy peak so strange and glorious that Petrarch climbed it to discover the view. Such activities were so unheard-of at the time that he is called the father of alpinism.

In order to make this trip, I had to learn to drive a standard-shift car, the only kind of car you could rent in France in those days. I am from the Bronx, and I am not what you would call a natural driver, but I like to drive. I find a school and explain my situation. "No problem, Madame. Come back tomorrow at nine and we will show you how to do it." The next day, I climb a street lined with knotty plane trees to the school. It is summer in Provence; smells of rosemary, thyme, and boxwood fill the air. When I get into the driver's seat, I tell the teacher

10

how nervous I am and in particular how unhinging I find driving in the city. "But, Madame, it is easy to drive in the city, and it is safe. Everyone goes slowly. You can hurt a car a little, but normally not people." His ease, as much as his logic, cures me of my fear.

I take to the road with great pleasure. I think of the boyfriend I have left in New York in my apartment. He didn't say "No, don't go." He said "It is important that you do this work." Still, I vomit all night long before I leave him. Perhaps I don't want him to see how much I want to go. But now here I am driving a stick shift. I spin along the sparkling bauxite gorges of la Nesque, accented here and there by stands of midnight-green firs. I drop down into the valleys, and the robust yet gentle beauty of Provence unfolds. Its lavender fields and vineyards, its sunflowers, red earth, spiky cypresses, Roman arches and viaducts regale me. A glorious display of color and the fragility of civilizations. I remember that Simone de Beauvoir had her first teaching job here and hiked the rugged footpaths alone. I envy her bravery.

With my windows rolled down, I drive through Aix and Arles, Bonnieux and Roussillon. I am stunned at how exactly the colors are Cézanne's green, blue, and orange, just like the bisque-and-brown hills of Tuscany are precisely what you see in early Italian Renaissance painting. This metamorphosis of art into life thrills me. I'm the magician. I'm making it happen. Cézanne's paintings and the landscape slip into each other like lovers.

I send my boyfriend postcards. I am in love with him as I write. But when I return to Paris, I discover that he has been having an affair with one of his students in my house in New York. In *my bed*. My neighbors know. He even enlisted a girlfriend of mine as a coconspirator. They have all gone out together. My girlfriend reports this to me when she meets me in Paris. She is not sorry. She tells me how unhappy she was in New York, how much she needed their company. I'm supposed to feel sorry for her.

———

The reader will certainly laugh, or pity me, when I say that my experience, in Provence and then in Paris afterward, probably clinched my decision to move to France twenty years later. Seduction and betrayal, I'm afraid, is a trajectory I call home. Some abandonments are simple—my mother, slamming that car door and driving away. It was clean, complete. I could be angry at her for the rest of my life. But with my father, it was messy. My dancey, charming father, hands outstretched insinuatingly one minute, only to drop drowsily to his side the next; his head bobbing in my direction, eyes twinkling, then five minutes later running off after the next sure thing. I entered his dance on his terms, like a girl stepping into a twirling jump rope. But there was no exit. I could only repeat the steps over and over and over again.

I'm a lot like my father, I know that. For decades, I never stayed in one job or kept one boyfriend for long. Early in my teaching career in the Seventies, when my friend Wanda said I should be more committed to the college I was teaching in, I didn't know what she was talking about. I thought, well, she's a minister's daughter from a small New England town. "Belonging," to her, means belonging to a community glued by the cement of her father's authority, perhaps love. I'm from

New York, I said to myself, I don't need a small community, I need a big city with all its disorder and excitement. It never occurred to me that I'm my father's daughter too, and that he taught me to keep moving, just like the boxer he had been, like the man he was. Don't stop, just keep bobbing and weaving. The miracle is that I stuck to a profession, and that later I would stick to Ken. I was an art history professor for twenty-three years, and I've been married now to Ken for twenty-two. But after I married him and knew there wouldn't be any more boyfriends, I quit my job and left New York. For France. For my father. To keep moving.

———

I'm working on a book about my father and his brother when I move to Paris. Dad's brother Dave had gone to Spain in 1938 to fight in the Spanish Civil War. My dad now lives in Israel. The book unexpectedly turns into a tirade that I lose control over. Here's why: When Dave left New York, where his parents were still living, he lied to them and said he was going to work in the Catskills, in a hotel in Monticello. He left behind letters describing his life there, to be sent to them via my father. But when he arrived in Spain a few weeks later, he changed his mind and told them the truth in long confessional letters.

I discover these letters when I am a child, although I don't read them then. One winter afternoon when I am twelve and playing in my grandparents' attic with my brother, David, and some cousins, we force open a locked drawer that we shouldn't have. At the bottom lie the letters—already crumbling—some black-and-white photographs, and a harmonica. Half in Yiddish, half in English, my twenty-two-year-old uncle whom I never met had written on July 10, 1938, to his parents:

> I am sitting on a mountain among vineyards and olive trees covered with the blood of Spain. I am looking at the sunset and I weep, and weep and weep. I am crying with hot tears that are pouring out of my eyes and I don't want to stop that flow of tears. Because I think of my dear parents. The thought of the pain and anguish I cause you and the thought that you think of me while you are reading this letter. I cry because I could not kiss you before I left because I could not tell you where I was going and not explain why I was going and I could not tell you what Spain means to you and the whole world. I lied to you because of my false letters that were sent from a hotel in Monticello. . . . Dear parents, don't worry about me and don't cry. . . . I want that you should excuse me for the story about the hotel. . . . When I return from Spain to you, I will tell you the whole story and ask your forgiveness. . . . I just reminded myself that July 18th is my birthday and the best present I can get from you is a letter of your forgiveness and love. . . .

Dave never got that letter from his parents, for the simple reason that my father never gave Dave's letters to them. And not even he knows why. "I just forgot," he tells me.

Dave was killed by a sniper on August 20 of the same year. On special occasions, Grandma pinned to her dress the little insignia she received from the American brigade in Spain, the Abraham Lincoln Brigade, honoring her son. Neither she nor

Grandpa ever read the letters. They didn't have the heart to, afterward.

My book would come to nothing. My anger at my father poisoned it. I made his last years difficult, though, prying admission after admission from him, even bringing him back to a traumatic memory from his childhood. I left him to die with that.

———

Maybe I wanted a fresh start and that's why I moved to France. I did feel bored with my American history, my story in America. I probably wanted to unstick myself of its mess. The very thought of Paris was so light and sweet by comparison. And then, of course, there was the incomparable beauty of the city. And Ken and I have always loved to eat well. We fell in love across lunches of smoked fish and white wine, chicken with blueberries, lemon tarts. And we needed more space. Ken's a painter. We couldn't afford to move to a larger place in Manhattan, and, considering where I came from, I didn't want to move to the boroughs.

In the summer of 1999, we read an article in the *New York Times* comparing the prices of apartments in New York and Paris. Paris is a third cheaper. We get on a plane two weeks later, shop hard for ten days, and buy a small duplex in the Tenth Arrondissement near the Gare de l'Est. We also buy Ken a studio right across the courtyard for $20,000.

The summer after we buy the apartment, we move. In our new neighborhood, I pick out a café where I hope I will be able to write. It's a down-at-the-heels place on the corner of our street. A few columns glitter with oblong pieces of mirror, some broken, others missing. The colors of the walls are brown and tan. The city is quiet; it's August. The French are all gone, and tourists don't come to this neighborhood. When I go in, the owners greet me politely—Claude, originally from the Auvergne, and his wife, Celeste, a Parisian. He's drying glasses, staring off into space; she's surveying the café's small outdoor terrace. At first, I just stop by for coffee, but soon I ask if I can bring my computer. Celeste says, "Of course, but you will have to come after lunch. We need all the tables at lunchtime."

The weeks go by and my work goes well. Different spots in the café appeal to me on different days. People come and go, temperature and light change. It's a neighborhood, the real world. Celeste, a large woman with smiling blue eyes, always has an encouraging word. She doesn't let anyone disturb me. *"Bon courage,"* she says when I begin each day. Good luck. She's motherly, and that appeals to me. The coffee is delicious. So are the white Sancerre wine and sausages Ken and I eat there together in the evening.

Claude and I rarely speak. Celeste says he doesn't hear well. He sings a lot, though, and when he's not singing, he has his opinions. About World War II and about Algeria, where he was a soldier and where, I suspect, he learned about cruelty that he could get away with. Claude appreciates Americans. He remembers how we helped the French at the end of the war. But mostly he burnishes his memories of Charles de Gaulle. Claude loves the grandeur of France. What France used to be, he says. Each day he makes sure that my table is just so, and when it's hot he gives me extra ice for my Perrier.

Docs Claude fantasize, when he remembers de Gaulle, that he would himself have been a Resistance fighter? That he would have been among the very small number of French people who stood up to the Nazis? The French have been very successful at convincing themselves and the world that they hated them. They didn't do anything wrong on their own, they say; the Germans forced them.

But the truth is that the French police were better, for example, at rounding up Jews than the Germans. They didn't even need the SS in Paris. When the French turned their backs on the French Jews, they were perhaps expressing what they had always felt—even after 1791, when the postrevolutionary National Assembly had made Jews citizens of France. *Fraternité* or no *fraternité*, Jews were not French at all. And France, as Jean-Marie Le Pen—leader of the fascist party, the National Front—says today, is for the French, and he means the European-born French: *"Les Français d'abord."*

I notice that when an African peddler covered with jangling beads, scarves, and purses comes into the café, Claude calls him Mamadou. The next day when another African stops by, he is Mamadou, too. Then I hear Claude calling all his Arab customers Mohammed. If they come in alone, that is. If they arrive in a group he serves them silently and retreats to a corner.

So, Claude, I say to myself, would you have called Ken and me David and Sarah during World War II? Or would you have called us something worse? Do you and your sweet, friendly wife vote fascist, Monsieur?

I'm astonished at how angry I am.

One day Claude says to me, "Do you remember the war,

Madame? Oh yes, of course you do," he answers. "Me too," he continues, "I remember," and he breaks into the song "It's a Long Way to Tipperary." Earlier he had been singing a Chevalier tune. He doesn't seem to discriminate. First a song the Allies—the Brits—sang, then a song by a collaborator. What kind of Victory Day was it for you, Claude, I wonder. Were you on a farm somewhere in the Auvergne, a small boy doing chores for your mother, when the news came through? Were your parents overjoyed? Did they toss their baby boy up in the air, elated, as my father did me in front of his luncheonette, confetti streaming down? Or did your parents weep for the loss of their German friends?

Of course, it is my own paranoia that pushes me toward these elaborate fantasies. The Auvergne was in Vichy, the Unoccupied Zone of France. There wouldn't have been many Germans around. The casual anti-Semitism I suspect in Claude doesn't mean his family liked the Nazis' policies toward Jews. And even if they did, they may still have hated the Germans for invading their country and humiliating them. Anti-Semitism didn't necessarily mean support of the Nazis. Nor did opposition to them always mean opposition to anti-Semitism. But for me, now making my home in France, French history and reality paradoxically drift away.

Still, whatever my mixed feelings about Claude and the French, I want his attention, and his courteousness. I try to engage him. I want him to like me, to see how wonderful Jews are and what a mistake he's made—as if I'm certain he's made this particular mistake. I'm not sure I like Claude, but I want him to like me. I want to be able to trust him. I don't want to be afraid of him. There's the truth of it: I don't want to be afraid. And it's sixty years after the Holocaust.

—

I think I've come to France to remember what I learned with
Philippe, and in Provence and in Notre Dame. I've come to
slow my life down, to be happy. I've come out of respect for
France's great radical tradition, their Revolution and their
democratic Republic—all that I had learned about as a child
and, in a way, all that my uncle had died for in Spain: Liberty,
Equality, Fraternity. And I've come for my father. So why am I
so angry? Didn't I know the French were anti-Semites? Everybody else knows.

After my research trip to Provence all those years ago, I
begin to write about Degas and his friend Valernes. I am so
seduced—so ennobled, I want to say—by the Provençal landscape, and by the intelligence of Degas's work, that I ignore his
anti-Semitism. I write a book about him and never mention it.
But now that I live in France, I've discovered that the glorious
Vaucluse is the heart of the French fascist party. "Arab, go
home," they say. And in Carpentras, where Jews have lived
since as long ago as the Middle Ages—albeit as pariahs until
the French Revolution—the Jewish cemetery has been defaced
regularly since 1990. I'd heard about it. Where did I put this
information?

Today, French Sephardic Jews tell me they are called *"sale
juif"*—dirty Jew—in the street. Sweet girls with their mothers,
young men with their girlfriends, a boy walking home alone
from school are subjected to this humiliation. An acquaintance upstairs, a Catholic French man and gay activist, proud
of his long stay in North America and exquisitely sensitive to
homophobia, tells me about Sephardic Jewish women he

worked with in Montreal. They were so showy and over-dressed, he says. *You just knew they were Jewish.*

Another neighbor, Armand Bertrand, is a large, nasty man who has a construction business in our building. He uses his body to threaten people. Often he parks his van illegally outside my window. I decide to leave a note taped to his windshield wiper asking him to move the truck. An hour later, a terrific pounding on my door jolts me out of my seat. I'm too afraid to respond. When Ken comes home, he finds that Bertrand has attached the note I had written to him to our door. Soon after, he or his son glues our locks, starts ringing our doorbell at 5 A.M., deposits dog shit on our doorstep. He is the man who screams into our Muslim concierge's face, "I don't like Arabs," and whose sidekick threatens him with a gun. The concierge quits.

I hear a young writer discuss his first novel at a large book fair in Paris. He mentions the Jewish scientists who invented the atom bombs that were dropped on Hiroshima and Nagasaki. He says, "How ironic that Jews did that after suffering at the hands of the Nazis." No one challenges him. No one asks why he blames the Jewish scientists and not the American government. A friend tells me that this kind of thing happens more and more these days. "Anti-Semitism is acceptable again," she says. There is a law against hate speech in France, but the writer I hear doesn't feel that what he is mouthing is hate speech. He thinks it's the simple truth. He is an anti-Semite.

France today has the largest Muslim population—at five million—in Europe. Since the start of the Palestinian Second Intifada in 2000 and the attacks on the World Trade Towers in

New York in 2001, France is nervous about antagonizing their Arab population, though at the same time they continue their exclusionary behavior toward them. Because of this contradiction, France has shied away from dealing with Arab anti-Semitism, which is the most virulent form of prejudice against Jews in France today, and is expressed both toward Israel and verbally on the streets toward Sephardic Jews. This situation has given certain French Catholics permission to express their own long-held anti-Semitic prejudices.

I have begun to wonder why so very few of the French monuments to World War II use the word "Jew" when they memorialize the hundreds of thousands murdered in the camps? Because their heroes, the Resistance fighters, along with the Communists and trade unionists, died because of what they *chose* to be—while the Jews only died because of who they *were?* No special valor there? Is that what the French think? And yes, I know it's not *all* French people, but against my better judgment I step into these crude oversimplifications. Just as they do.

———

Like Claude, my dad worked behind a counter. Everybody loved his luncheonette, the morning aromas, the hot coffee and fresh Danish, the sizzling bacon and eggs. He was happy, wrapped in his white apron, gliding here and there. He had heard of the Nazi massacres near his home in Riga, the stampeding and screaming in the forest nearby, the pits where Jews were gunned down and covered over. My father was lucky he escaped. And I? I have gone back to Europe?

I walk the French streets, hike the mountains, marvel at the curves of mansard roofs, the grace of wrought-iron balconies, and then I learn that the people who live here and produce this refined culture vote fascist in startling numbers. And that France was the only conquered nation whose government officially collaborated with the Germans. And ten years after that, tortured and massacred Arabs in Algeria and in Paris. In November 2005, the mostly Muslim suburbs rioted, exploding in their rage toward a racist government and racist culture that continues to wrap itself in the rhetoric—but not the behavior—of French revolutionary values. So, why am I here?

When Ken brings home that warm, crunchy baguette for breakfast, and we try to resist the fresh farm butter and fail, we think "Well, yes, that's why we're here." We love being physically pampered and alive in all our senses all the time. The crêpes on the street, the roasting chickens, the cheeses, the tarts, the perfumed men and women. These are aromas that you don't simply inhale and forget. They infiltrate your soul. You remember them and long for them. Proust didn't come from nowhere. He was a French man. A half-Jewish French man.

When I gaze out my office window into our courtyard that looks like a village street, I think "Yes, that's why." The graceful bridges spanning the lazy twisting Seine, the glory of Notre Dame, *and* the taxes French people pay are all reasons why I'm here. France taxes the rich to pay for daycare, universal health coverage, a constant round of flower plantings all year long in parks all over the city. Taxes support artists and the great French film industry. In France, there is a working population that can pull off a general strike and stop the country cold. That's the nation I've chosen to live in, too. Doesn't that make sense?

~

The last time I see my father is in Natanya, Israel, in 2001. He is eighty-nine years old. When I pick up my bags to leave, he is sitting at a little desk near the door, fiddling with some papers. He looks at me vaguely and, in a shaky voice, says "So you moved to Paris. Why did you do that, Euniska?"

CHAPTER 1

Mother

It starts on a winter's morning. At eight it's still nighttime, dark outside and cold. I hug myself in the corner of our small kitchen at the long wooden table, waiting for my coffee. Ken turns on the espresso machine and pre-heats the bowls. He loads the coffeemaker and foams the milk. He pushes the button and fills each bowl halfway up. Then he spoons in the whipped white froth. I look out the window at the hotel across the street whose shabby façade, inexplicably, sports two Renaissance sculptures, an Adonis and a Venus. Cupping my hands around my bowl—they barely reach, so round and deep and plush is this extravagant invention—I look at Ken. I'm content.

Many French people begin their days this way, with their hands around mammalian bowls. I know I will never need anything more to make me strong and happy. Ingmar Bergman surely had this in mind in the final scenes of *Cries and Whispers*, when a maid takes her dying mistress to her breast, offering her what all the world longs for all our lives. That first and complete experience of compassion that is mother-love. Yes, I want the sensual pleasures of Paris even as a baby wants its mother's body, her sweet voice, her dear flesh.

The French guiltlessly satisfy their sensual urges all day long. They may forget appointments, but they never forget their senses. They are not purposeful in this behavior; it is simply who they are. An ancient commandment calls across their bodies: Before all else, thou shalt eat, touch, listen, smell, and see.

In 1996, when President François Mitterrand, a great gourmand, was near death, he invited close friends to a New Year's dinner. He consumed three dozen oysters and two ortolans. These tiny migrating birds, an endangered species that French people nowadays are forbidden to eat, are stuffed with foie gras, then roasted. French experts call them "the world's most succulent delicacy." They are eaten in one mouthful. When the dish arrived at the table, Mitterand and all his guests spread their linen napkins over their heads and devoured the birds in ecstatic, illicit privacy.

Even my plumber in Paris has culinary opinions and wants to discuss them, and so does the man who comes to fix my stove. We debate the differences between Brie de Meaux and Brie de Melun. The former, larger and flatter, is milder, and some would say more delicate and refined. The latter is thicker and a bit saltier, perhaps more robust. This preoccupation with food that almost amounts to an obsession is not limited to people of European French descent. In Paris, Senegalese, Mauritians, Indians, and Moroccans all celebrate their national specialties. Someone recalls a smooth and creamy potato gratin, someone else the sea-brininess of an oyster dug up in the Arcachon beds near Bordeaux. Then there's a fragrant lamb tagine from Fez, a cardamom- and coriander-rich lentil dal from Pakistan, and the silken, alpine-infused Mont d'Or cheese from the Franche-Comté. Mont d'Or is a New Year's Eve specialty, warmed in the oven until it runs, then served in the middle of the table with spoons for everyone. Big spoons.

I shake my head in disbelief. This hedonism must be bad for them. But no, they're doing fine. They live longer lives than Americans do, are more productive for hours worked, rank number three among exporters worldwide, are the fourth biggest economic power. Pleasure doesn't seem to slow them down. They are not dying of it. Any more than I did when my grandparents' house in Hurleyville filled with smells of chicken soup flavored with dill and carrots, omelets scrambled in brown butter, sautéing breaded veal cutlets. The pleasure of good food only added to my happiness at not being in the Bronx with my parents. It was going home that was deadly.

My father may have urged me to go to France, but he would never understood French appetites. One of his favorite dictums was "You don't live to eat, you eat to live." I cannot recall a time when he tasted something and said "That's terrific." Not my grandmother's mashed potatoes and pot roast, nor the skirt steak and tsimmis (a delicious mixture of carrots, sweet potatoes, and raisins), not even a hot pastrami sandwich. He never ate the chocolates he sold in his parents' shop, he said, and he never brought me a sundae from his candy store. He enjoyed a shot of rye, though, picked up the tiny glass, weighed it in the palm of his hand, tossed it down smacking his lips, proud like the kid who drags on a cigarette and successfully exhales for the first time.

Once when I cooked for him he said, "That was good," followed quickly with "Well, if you can read, you can cook." "You're a good reader, Pop," I joked, "what happened to your cooking skills?"

If there is one thing that people know about Marcel Proust's *In Search of Lost Time*, it is a small French pastry called a madeleine, which appears at the end of the "Overture" to *Swann's Way*. Proust wrote:

> One day in winter, on my return home, my mother, seeing that I was cold, offered me some tea, a thing I did not ordinarily take. I declined at first, and then, for no particular reason, changed my mind. She sent for one of those squat, plump little cakes called "petites madeleines". . . . I raised to my lips a spoonful of the tea in which I had soaked a morsel of the cake. No sooner had the warm liquid mixed with the crumbs touched my palate than a shudder ran through me and I stopped, intent upon the extraordinary thing that was happening to me. An exquisite pleasure had invaded my senses. . . . And at once the vicissitudes of life had become indifferent to me. . . .

Proust was not exactly a happy man, but still. . . . Who knows what that ice-cream sundae might have done for me, and a stolen chocolate or two for my father? At least we might have become literary geniuses. Instead we drove ourselves nuts in New York. We'd walk from his furniture store—the last (and, finally, a successful one!) of his many businesses—on Upper Broadway down to a Jewish Deli on Seventy-eighth Street. Arm in arm, a seventeen-year-old girl and her father, we enjoyed the city. Like two penguins dressed correctly, we turned this way and that, always in unison, always in accord. The comfort of our agreement swept me down the street. But at some point, my father would make fun of a kid's haircut or his sloppy clothing. "I'm glad I don't have such problems with my children," he'd say, implying God help us if he did. That was my cue to tell him what a terrific parent he was, and how alike we were in every little thing. I did it, but I also took my arm out of his, and dropped my hands into my pockets. He'd sensed that we were no longer in sync. He'd noticed a man selling jewelry from a stand on the street, and spit out "New York is really going to the dogs; it didn't used to be like this."

By the time we got to the deli, I'd lost my appetite. I hesitated between the ordinary but delicious rare roast beef sandwich and what I knew my father thought was the better choice, hot pastrami on rye. I ordered hot pastrami. We both got potato salad and cream sodas.

In my eyes, my father was confident, unassailable even if I noticed that he took a lot of pills for a heart condition no doctor could locate. He was moody, too, and strict. It took so little to make him angry. Maybe he felt guilty about coming to America and leaving all the Jews to die in Riga. Or maybe he had the immigrant's distrust of the great good life in this brand-new country. Or maybe he shuddered at America's relentless push to make more and more money.

He did go home again, though, after divorcing my mother when I was in my mid-twenties. He married his cousin from Riga, she with her Russian poetry, slender figure, and stylish clothes. Off he went like a bullet. But that was to Israel, not to Europe. I stayed in New York with my mother. Until I moved to France.

It's our first New Year's in Paris, and a friend arrives late in the evening with the woman he is planning to marry. The man, Christophe, pulls up a chair next to mine. As Ken prepares the cheese platter, Christophe leans toward me in a way that says "What I have to say is only for you." He picks up some gaily colored ribbons discarded on the table and distractedly makes little bracelets. He winds them around and around my wrist. This intimacy is so casual and so pleasant, the touch of his fingers, the hair on his arms peeking out of his cuffs, his smell.

During a documentary about the end of World War II, I notice that every time austere, aristocratic Charles de Gaulle meets someone, he touches the person's shoulder or arm, clasps the hand that offers the bouquet of flowers. My father was like that. He surprised Ken when they first met by the way his fingers rested on his son-in-law's arm, or how he circled his shoulders, or brushed a crumb from his jacket. My father loved Ken, who reminded him of his father.

I always enjoyed looking at my dad's body. All my lovers have been like him—lean, hard, elegant. As a kid, I waited for him to get up in the morning so I could watch him. I'd sit on the windowsill in the room I shared with my brother, which looked into the living room where my parents slept. I waited and waited, and then it happened. I'd see him pulling one leg, then the other, out from under the covers. He'd stand, his shorts hanging low. He pulled them up and moved drowsily to the bathroom. I could almost smell him. (I've heard that you fall in love with people because their smell suits you.) He doused his face with cold water, washed his hands, cleaned his nails. He smiled in the mirror.

My dad and I were never in a room together where he was not touching me. Unless he was angry. Then all bets were off, and he might never touch me again. Frantically, I'd try to mend whatever it was I'd broken. My hands shook, my spine tingled. What could I do? What had I done?

I read a psychiatric case report once about a woman suffering from severe depression that only sets in when her husband, a naval officer, leaves to go on duty for several months. She becomes listless, losing all desire to do anything. She tells her psychiatrist that she doesn't mind being unhappy when her husband leaves, but what she can't stand is that when he "disappears," so does she. That's how I felt about my father. That if he stopped hugging me, kissing me, taking my arm, I would disappear.

It never occurred to me that I could walk away or get angry, until the day he insulted Ken. We were all on the steps of Avery Fisher Hall at Lincoln Center, where we had just been to the opera. He reached for me. I avoided him. He said, "Don't make a big deal out of nothing. I was just telling Ken the truth," and his fingers lengthened toward me again. "Maybe it's time to think twice before you display your talent for honesty," I said with newfound confidence, and walked away. That was that for ten years. What a relief it was not to see or speak to him. To this day, I don't understand why I ever renewed our contact.

I don't have the same problem with my mother. We aren't physically intimate. Once, we must have been, but I can't remember. After she left me in the Catskills with my grandparents, I wouldn't touch her again. Perhaps I couldn't bear the reminder of what she had taken away, or the longing her body triggered in me. I've seen my friends with their infants: Kay with Juliet, Muriel with Nino. You can taste their complicity. My mother must have felt something of that tenderness toward me.

⁓

The French always seem to be touching something—each other, a cigarette, a wine glass. Their hands are busy and beautiful. Sometimes I think they can't tell the difference between your body and theirs, that what they need is endless stimulation and connection.

It never stops. You go to the bank. People are in line. Within two minutes, the man behind you knocks into your shoulder without apology. The arm of the woman in front of you leans into your ribs. It feels like a line-up for a relay race.

In the Métro, it's more of the same—shoulder-to-shoulder, arm-to-arm, nose-to-nose. Even if the car is not crowded, you are plunged into other people's bodies. The seats are narrow and in most cases you face one another—you can't avoid it—and your knees touch, especially when you sit down and when you leave. Inevitably you knock into the person opposite or get tangled in handbags, newspapers, briefcases, and scarves. Especially if you're American, because no matter how slim you are, you seem bigger than they are, physically more unwieldy. And they don't make it easier for you; they don't get out of your way. If it were New York, you'd recoil or say something rude. Here, you just stay put. You're keeping each other company, like the saints lined up on the façade of Notre Dame. Or the angels crowded onto the top of column capitals holding up the roof. Nobody's alone in French churches, or on French streets, or in the cafés. Even on a wide-open highway, French drivers tailgate maniacally.

———

I come to Paris like a mongrel sniffing her way across the Atlantic. When I arrive as a student, the first smell that startles me is body odor. No smell is so repulsive to Americans. Soon, though, it joins the parade of all the other smells— coffee, butter-drenched pastries, peanuts spinning in sugar, perfume.

In New York, I put my broccoli on the table. Very green, but flavorless. Then there's orange for carrots, and red for peppers. Or blue cheese that's blue but only tastes of chemicals. Forget the bread. Food in America is like the color-drenched pictures in a child's dictionary. Just color. Then I move to France, and all those flat forms and saturated hues pop up out of the page and regale me with their textures, aromas, tastes.

In markets, indoors and out, peaches, pears, apples, roasting chickens, barbecuing pork, silver, white, red, and blue fish from all the rivers and seas of France, heave themselves at you. Flowers of every size and color dare you to touch them, bury your head in them. Sour and intimate aromas thicken the air in the cheese shop, as ancient odors of churning milk come strangely close to bodily smells. It's only food, I say to myself. Take it easy. But I can't. Ken and I look at each other ecstatically and laugh. And laugh and laugh. What a nice life.

All day long, I feel other people's cheeks on mine as I kiss my friends hello and goodbye on both sides of their face, lingering as long as I like. I smell them, look at the color of their eyes, their hair. My social life is lived across my body in a way I could never have imagined.

I left New York looking for pleasure, but I had no idea the extent to which the French are in the thrall of their senses and how they do not hesitate to satisfy them. They're like babies, and it doesn't take me long to realize that I want exactly what they want.

—

I did covet that ice-cream sundae from my father's fountain, and my mom hid the cookies because she said we were eating too many. She was, anyway. My father said we were all gaining weight except him, and particularly my mother. He hated that. Still, he walked around our apartment half naked and her pajamas were always torn. They must have been having sex.

We lived on top of each other in those few rooms. My brother and I slept five feet apart. When he broke my records, I wanted to kill him. He was only six years old. My anger silently accumulated and I'd end up ripping the sleeve out of the socket of a friend's dress when I didn't even know I was upset. I was just trying to get her attention, and the next thing I knew her sleeve was in my hand and she was crying. Intensity steamed off of our apartment. All the senses were alarmed all the time. But it wasn't friendly.

In France, the senses call you to life too, but sweetly, caressingly, one sense calmly coupling with the next. Even the children know.

Ken and I go to see *Before Sunset* with Viva, the nineteen-year-old daughter of our friend Brigitte. In the film, an American man and a French woman, who haven't seen each other for ten years and never expected to again, meet in a bookstore where the man is reading from his first novel. The book recounts the day they spent together in Vienna ten years earlier, the day they met and fell in love—a day portrayed in a previous film, *Before Sunrise*. That day, when the girl boards a train for home, they promise to meet again in six months. In the second film, we learn that they did not. *Before Sunset* takes place in real time as the two try to discover each other's and their own feelings. Both have been bruised over the previous ten years. Dreaming is no longer what it was. He is unhappily married and worries that he is throwing his life away in boring routines. She likes her work but has not found the partner she hoped for. Now and then during the few hours they are together, he drapes his arm around her shoulders, she rests her hand on his. He brushes her hair from her forehead, her fingers flit across his arm. In fits and starts, not knowing anything for sure, they touch each other.

They take a boat up the Seine toward where the man has to catch his ride to the airport. Unexpectedly, he turns to her and says "Show me where you live." "But do you have time?" she asks. They walk to her apartment. Passing through the court-yard, they find her neighbors preparing a communal dinner. They are invited and nod awkwardly. They climb the stairs to her flat where she sings him a song that he requests, a song she mentioned earlier in the day. This is where the film ends.

I say to Ken and Viva, "Well, they're going to get into bed and stay there for a few days." Viva, our French girl, says, "No, they're going downstairs to eat with her neighbors." She knows in her bones what we do not: that all the French senses go together in no particular hierarchy. Touching, eating, fucking, they are all part of the same thing, so there's no reason to be in a hurry. That's what makes the French so naturally sexy. Kids know their parents' bodies and each other's. Breasts are every-where. Sweet, pretty, promising. We Americans are puritanical by comparison and obsessed with sex. This was even evident in a video Ken made about Madame de Pompadour and her lover, Louis XV. To suggest the sensuality of their relationship, he kept panning to their lime-green brocade-covered bed. A French person might have lingered on the china, the drapery, the views out the window.

It can't be an accident that the wilder and more imaginative forms of sexual pleasure are something we also associate with France. The Marquis de Sade, Pauline Réage's *The Story of O*, Georges Bataille. Pornography in France was seamlessly linked to social and political criticism and the freedom of expression produced by the French Revolution. Censorship never flourished there as it did in America and England. That's why books like Joyce's *Ulysses* and Henry Miller's *Tropic of Cancer* had to be published in France first. Even though my boyfriend Philippe was only half French, he was the only lover

I've ever had who suggested using pornographic literature in our lovemaking.

⁓

I am twelve years old. My father's cousin, the woman he will eventually make his second wife, arrives in New York from Israel. She starts buying me what she calls "tailored," "European" clothing. Tweed skirts, button-down shirts, leather belts. They might have been sexy on a European girl, but on me they are gloomy. My mother doesn't like them, and boys never ask me to dance. I don't believe my father when he says "Sweetheart, you're too smart for them." My mother says, honestly, "You're not that pretty." My father also says "You know, you really do look like my mother."

His mother, my mother. The mothers don't stop. My grandma trim, efficient, always side-by-side with Grandpa. And it's not just the photographs that make me think this. They were in business together, plotting all the time, enjoying themselves. And they were nice to each other, always convivial and amused, it seemed to me.

What a contrast with my parents. My father never let up on his ridicule of my mother's body. Why did he marry her? She was always round, just as she was always friendly and talked to strangers. He wanted her slim and all to himself. She told me once that she couldn't be too affectionate with me and my brother, because Daddy would be jealous. My mother always loved food. She will sample anything when she visits Ken and me in France, just as in the 1950s she got excited about trying deep-fried, honey-batter-dipped shrimp and salad with blue cheese dressing. Sometimes I think it was my mother's sheer self-indulgence that my father couldn't tolerate. She was large and sensual, the earthy presence in the house to be side-stepped. She never said No to herself. She did to us, but not to herself. He, on the other hand, ranneth over with Nos.

What did she get from the pleasure she took? She was fat, wasn't she? Or was she? Maybe she was just nicely plump or just not skinny. And as my dear friend Kay says, "There are a lot worse things in the world you can be than overweight. You could be a liar or a murderer or an anti-Semite." My father's disdain was catching, though. I was going to be slim like him.

Men liked my mother. I could see that on the subway and on buses. I doubt if she slept with anyone, though, while she was still with my father. I know Dad's brother Dave loved and trusted her. He wrote to his parents from Spain: "We need food not clothing. . . . Ask Trudy to find out where to send packages. . . . I am not sure of the address, but Trudy can find out."

Yes, ask Trudy. You can count on her to get the job done. Her matter-of-fact demeanor, deep voice, cigarette-smoking busyness. Yet she never stopped wanting to get Valentine's Day cards. She grew up in the Bronx and Harlem, her father a fruit seller and philanderer, as they used to say, her mom an overweight *balabuster*, homemaker, for a large, extended family. My mother never expected much from life. But she wanted to have fun and good food, and she got it. She still does. She is a veritable force of nature.

On the streets of Paris eyes slide over and around you, lingering at your eyes. You realize that all your life you've looked away. The law is strict in America: No looking, no touching. Anything but gaze into a stranger's eyes. Eyes confess.

I watch the men glide along with shirts hanging just-so over their fine, not-overly muscular torsos. I admire the women sauntering with blouses, skirts, or trousers hugging their perfect hips and breasts. Paris is a fashion runway. The ease, the swing, the grace of it. Even the trees parade down streets and boulevards at perfectly calibrated rhythms.

I am ravished by loveliness in the city, entranced by the tracery of balconies, the proud slope of mansard roofs, the winding streets. I am beguiled by lace curtains at a window, the arrangement of flowers in a box, the balletic leap of bridges across rivers and canals. Is this what my father had in mind, sending me here? No, these pleasures would have eluded him, I think. He wouldn't have noticed the worn toy boats with their delicately faded sails drifting in the pond at the Luxembourg Gardens. It would have made him too sad. He'd stick to girls. For him the city, as he imagined it, was for romance, that kind of freedom, a place where, in his fantasies, he wasn't married and didn't have children.

But he was no bohemian, even if he proudly told me "My brother Dave said I looked like a poet." He was the son of bourgeois parents, who had slid into the working class. He had to have a wife and children and provide for them. It was his destiny. And he had to long, heart and soul, for another life. It was his malady. He imagined himself driving a convertible with the top down, or smoking in a Paris café, smiling at smiling women. In fact, he stayed in the Bronx for a long time, gambled at poker tables and at the races, and failed in several businesses. But he deposited his fantasies in me, shimmering piece by shimmering piece.

———

Ken buys flowers in the market, and he and the florist end up talking about circumcision. Somehow she knows he's Jewish. She asks if he thinks he's missing out on some pleasure. He shrugs, "How would I know?" Talk, talk, talk. It never stops. They look at each other constantly, they bump into each other everywhere, they talk to each other all day long and everywhere. The division between mind and body that is so fixed in Anglo-Saxon life doesn't figure for them. It's as different a language as French is from English.

At the newspaper store, the normally tacit proprietor mutters, "Oh, the heat! Yes, but you have to live with it, don't you? *Il faut le faire.*" Or I'm tapping out an article on my computer at my corner café, I look up, and a handsome young man bends toward me. "You a writer?" He asks. "Yeah," I say. "Writers write in Paris cafés, don't they?" "Only Americans think that," he says, smiling, condescending—Oh, you Americans do romanticize us—but flirtatious, an invitation to meet, to play.

A couple of days later, he and his girlfriend, Gilles and Brigitte, invite us over for a drink. They live in a duplex penthouse apartment that she owns. A large terrace overlooks shabby rue du Faubourg St. Denis. But if you look out, across the city, what you see is shimmering, silver-gray Paris with its curving roofs, clusters of stubby terra-cotta chimneys, floor-to-ceiling windows. The Eiffel Tower surveys the city from the horizon.

We start drinking at about eight on the terrace amidst bamboo and olive trees, bougainvillea, roses, and a string of little colored lights hung above the table. Brigitte—tall, graceful Brigitte in a black sleeveless T-shirt and jeans, who I learned later rarely cooks—nonchalantly, with a cigarette dangling from her lips, carries out plate after plate of olives and sliced sausages, savory puff pastries, luscious Brie de Meaux and Montbriac accompanied by a crusty country bread filled with nuts and raisins. Later there's an apricot tart. Ken is sure that we drink four bottles of Champagne. Like a magic fairy, Brigitte keeps it flowing. You wouldn't want to interrupt by asking to help.

What a wild ride we have that night into French and American movies. Brigitte is an actress, Gilles a director. We rush at the films and each other in a delirium of articulateness. Friction, play, combativeness set the tone. Making an argument doesn't interest the French as much as piling up dazzling observations. It's a performance, a drama. Our new friends don't look for conciliation, or a smooth ride. On the contrary, they like it bumpy, meandering, provocative, like making love. It's the patter of the language that amuses them, the theater of their lives, the moment-to-moment connecting of one person to another through language and glances piled on fantasy and projection, running in and out and around their senses and all that great food Brigitte offers us.

We all love Bertolucci's *Conformist, 1900*, and *Last Tango*; Coppola's *Godfather*, Parts One and Two, but *not* Three; Scorsese's *Taxi Driver* and *Raging Bull*. They are fans of Howard Hawks.

Mme de Staël, writing from unhappy exile in Germany in the early nineteenth century, said, "The feeling of satisfaction

that characterizes an animated conversation does not so much
consist of its subject matter. . . . Rather, it is a certain manner
in which some people have an effect on others; of reciprocally
and rapidly giving one another pleasure. . . ." Exactly what we
are doing that evening.

Ken and I fall over ourselves and out of the building at 2 A.M.
"Do you think they liked us as much as we liked them?" I ask.
"Will they call us?"

A week later we learn that they're splitting up. I'm devastated. When I run into Brigitte I weep, and I hardly know her.
She says with her great, glamorous hauteur, "Ça va"—the "ah"
of "va" pulled all the way out. It's okay. "We've been talking
about it for a long time." The two of them seemed so engaged
with each other. Maybe I wasn't looking closely. Or maybe they
were that engaged. Gilles is married now in America, but he
stays in contact with Brigitte.

———

Sometimes, when I'm having a good time writing, I stop dead
in mid-sentence. A psychiatrist once said to me, "Be careful
about getting overexcited. It's not good for you." I nodded my
head, understanding that I mustn't want too much, dive in,
swim, that it will make me ill. Or I'll explode and disappear.
The more one wants, the more one can lose. But the longer I
live in France, the more I think that sensual and intellectual
contentment at a high pitch—at the "overexcited" level—is
exactly what keeps the French going. Why not me, too?

One day Brigitte asks me, "Do you know why we clink
glasses when we drink?"

"No," I answer.

"It's to add a lovely sound to the pleasures of color and smell and taste."

Of course it is.

The coddling never stops. The French really are a bunch of babies disguised as adults. But they are not in a stupor. They are not drooling over their café tables, or sleeping their days away. I jerk along from one project to the next, twisted up in my boring tribulations, and they are touching, tasting, seeing, and fucking each other all day long.

"Never mind, darling," Paris says, "I'm good for you. I promise, you can be as overexcited as you like!"

France is that invitation to live, to have my mother's appetite. Maybe even, finally, to have my mother.

———

I often dine with English friends in Paris who despise the French and hate living there. Stuart is a journalist covering France for a year, Kay a novelist. They complain that all the women tie their scarves the same way. That whatever you order in a restaurant, the waiter sneers at you. That Parisians forever bang into you on the street. And that the French have no sense of humor. And why, my friends practically shriek, do they need so many cheeses? This, at the pitch of Rex Harrison's *cri de coeur* in *My Fair Lady*: "Why can't a woman be more like a man?"

There certainly is an awful lot of dairy produced in France. A dizzying array of yogurts and mousses, and a constant stream of newly invented hybrids fill the supermarkets. Then there's milk, butter, cream, and cheese. But it's when I wander into the back of a market that the full impact of French dairy production hits me. Piled to the ceiling is a mountain of long-shelf-life milk—whole, semi-skimmed, and skimmed. I never saw so much milk in one place in my life. The French, it turns out, are massive closet milk-drinkers.

I mention this to my Franco-phobic friend Stuart, who happens—one wouldn't want to wander in the twists and turns of his psyche—to also adore Proust and a lot else that's French. He smiles and says, "Wait until you hear about Proust and milk." One Proust expert, he tells me, says that milk in *In Search of Lost Time* is always associated with peace of mind.

"Well," I say, "for whom does milk *not* represent peace of mind? Mother's milk. It's obvious."

But then Stuart tells me about a passage in which the character Charles Swann climbs a grand staircase lined with liv-eried attendants, thinking how much happier he'd be ascending the dark smelly stairs to the apartment of the little dressmaker friend of his lower-class lover. He would sit and talk with the dressmaker and so bring himself closer to his lover. He recalls how at night on those humble stairs an empty, unwashed milk can is set out on every doormat.

"That's interesting," I say, "but really, milk-cans, milk-bot-tles, milk-cartons tumble through all our memories."

Finally Stuart brings home his point. Proust is on a train that makes a stop between two mountains. Down in the gorge he sees a "tall girl . . . emerge from the house, and, climbing a path lighted by the first slanting rays of the sun, come toward the station carrying a jar of milk. . . . She passed down the line of windows, offering coffee and milk to a few awakened passengers. Flushed with the glow of morning, her face was rosier than the sky. I felt on seeing her that desire to live which is reborn in us whenever we become conscious anew of beauty and of happiness. . . . Life would have seemed an exquisite thing to me if only I had been free to spend it, hour after hour, with her, to go with her to the stream, to the cow, to the train, to be always at her side, to feel that I was known to her, had my place in her thoughts."

One can only imagine what Proust's life would have been like had his fantasy been satisfied. But still this scene is one of primordial joy, an infant at its mother's breast—the "tall girl," the "first slanting rays of the sun," the "offering" of milk, the "glow," the "happiness." To stay by her side all day long—forever.

Proust certainly would not have written his great book had he climbed off the train that day. Not to mention how surprised the girl would have been. Still, the milk and the simple, and simply beautiful, milkmaid *might* have brought Marcel eternal contentment. That's what Proust hopes, and, my God, so do we.

I have always been a huge milk-drinker. But I don't think I've ever had strong feelings about breasts, one way or the other. I do recall being fascinated, however, as only a little Jewish girl could be, by nuns who, when I was young, still dressed in their strict black-and-white garb. I was particularly struck by the fact that they appeared to have no breasts. I remember an experience I had when I was about five years old, riding on a trolley with my mother. The seats were woven laminated straw; thick brown leather straps hung down from above. A nun got on and sat opposite us. Her black tunic filled the seat. Her kind face peeked out from her stiff white headdress, which wrapped across her forehead and under her chin and held her head firmly above her wide white collar. She had no hair. She had no body. She was very white. "Mommy, what's the matter with her?" I asked. "Nothing's the matter, darling," my mother said, straightening my dress. "Why does she look like that?" My mother turned to the nun and said, "Excuse my daughter, Sister, she has never seen a nun before. We're Jewish." That's when I stretched my hand out to touch the nun's chest. My mother, aghast, pulled my hand down, and yanked me off the trolley at the next stop.

———

What is one to make of the 350 cheeses fabricated all over France? Yes, France is an agriculturally rich country and has been for centuries, but not every country so endowed becomes the world's greatest cheese creator and purveyor. The French fight no battle in the European Union more intensely than the campaign to protect their cheeses, particularly against a ban on the unpasteurized milk that is fundamental to their insinuating tastes and textures.

Of course, Americans like cheese, too. We have our "American cheese" and "Philadelphia cream cheese." We have cheeseburgers, grilled cheese sandwiches, and macaroni and cheese. Some people even pull Jarlsberg and Brie from the imported cheese case in their supermarkets. But no uninitiated American could possibly be prepared for the array of cheeses that greets her near the end of every dinner in a French friend's home. You begin to lust for cheese as much as you do for the dessert that will surely follow.

The French have marvelous complexions and the longest lives in the Western world despite their smoking, meat and fat consumption, and drinking. Maybe it's the milk. *Or maybe it's the mothers.* Maybe Proust is not the only French person transfixed by his mother.

The place of mothering women in French culture, symbolically and in reality, is indeed prodigious. In France, an army of women waits to help you at every turn. Pharmacies are almost as numerous in France as bakeries, and most of the pharmacists are women. Serious, knowledgeable, and maternal, they patiently respond to every question, no matter how intimate or complicated. It's the first place I go when I get nervous about bird flu. They deal with mysterious maladies or ordinary ones—headaches, stomach pain, backache, palpitations, sleeplessness, anguish. Every woe of the body—including sagging skin—is taken seriously. It's normal to go to a pharmacy and ask for help. Pharmacists work marvels, just like the doctors, who also are usually women.

I visit the doctor, and the first thing I notice is that there's no receptionist. I enter a simple waiting room. A few minutes later, the doctor appears. She's dressed like me, no white coat. She doesn't call me by my given name, that demeaning American habit. There's nothing authoritarian about her. Nor do dollar or euro signs light up her eyes. She's in no rush. I sit down; she waits for me to tell her what the problem is. Afterward, she asks me questions and by her pace invites me to respond carefully and precisely. Then she examines me. She is exacting and matter-of-fact. She is not asking for admiration. She's motherly. I trust her.

She tells me, "You don't become a doctor in France to make a lot of money." Then we fall into conversation about the nineteenth century. "It was the worst century for women," she says. I wouldn't have taken her for a feminist. In any case, most historians would say the nineteenth century's many liberation movements planted the seeds of the women's movement. Does my doctor prefer pre-Revolutionary aristocratic France? I ask her. She gives me a wicked smile.

———

Even the French government is maternal. It spends fortunes on education, health care, unemployment insurance. It beautifies its cities for no other reason than to make their inhabitants happy and proud to be French. The poorest neighborhoods undergo constant refurbishing—broadening of streets, planting of trees and flowers, cleaning obscure monuments, lighting forgotten fountains. This is less the case, unfortunately, in the largely Muslim-populated suburbs.

We in America never expect much from the state for our cities. Good interstate highways are about all we want. It's as if New York potholes, garish L.A. advertisement, Detroit central-city blight, rundown subways in Buffalo and Chicago, make the cities the irritants we assume them to be. That's how we know we're alive in America. We manage, we figure things out, we're stoic, and we're smart. We're rich, aren't we? We're also hard, pushy, and angry. We shoot each other in obscene numbers. We are the only Western democracy that kills people for crimes they did or did not commit. And of course, we also abandon the poor, the old, and the sick. We are not motherly.

———

Around 1990, I am finishing a book about Edouard Manet's model, Victorine Meurent. It is giving me a lot of trouble, and I decide to start swimming every day. I'm not much of a swimmer, but I begin a daily regimen in a sparkling, blue-tiled pool on the far west side of Manhattan. A pitched glass roof covers the pool, and from one of the hot tubs I see the old McGraw-Hill building, proudly stepped and wrapped in its own watery-green glazed bricks and glass. Each day I do my laps, goggled and bathing-capped, snug in the cool aqua of the water, and, as it happens, accompanied by schools of plump naked females swimming alongside or lounging at the edge. I've conjured these voluptuous companions, who look like they are on sabbaticals from François Boucher's eighteenth-century paintings, to keep me company, help me finish my book. They cheer me on. France feels just like that swimming pool to me, filled to overflowing with motherly types.

It's true that my mother and I are not close the way some mothers and daughters are. We've never been really complicit. But we love each other. She's ninety now and lives in New York. Some would say I left her there when I moved to France. And, just before I left, she underwent serious surgery. Tubes led from all parts of her body, one pressed her beautiful, thick hair flat down on to her head. It ruined her—or me—the way she looked in that hospital bed. Every day I went to see her, and one day, I blurted out, "Mom, please don't leave me." And she said, "Don't worry, Eunice, I'm not going to leave you." But she looked at me again and said, "Well, someday I'll have to leave you." I sat there at the edge of her bed sobbing, and two weeks later I moved to France.

⁓

I know it's silly to reduce Proust's glorious evocation of a life and a time to a tormented love story about him and his mother. Rather like thinking of Martin Luther as hating his father so much that he decided to destroy the power of the biggest father on earth, the pope. Still, it's tempting. Who can forget the kiss at the beginning of *In Search of Lost Time?*

"I would have kissed Mamma then and there, but at that moment the dinner-bell rang. . . ."

Then his father says, "No, no, leave your mother alone. You've said good night to one another, that's enough. These exhibitions are absurd. Go on upstairs."

The boy mounts the "hateful staircase." He agonizes over ways to get his mother upstairs to him, to get his kiss. His desperation thickens. Will she come? Won't she? He knows she knows he's suffering.

We ache for him and for ourselves. We remember: waiting for the phone to ring, the e-mail to arrive. Waiting to be loved.

Proust continues, "I was stirred to revolt, and attempted the desperate stratagem of a condemned prisoner. I wrote to my mother begging her to come upstairs. . . ."

This scheme fails too.

"Then, suddenly," he writes, "my anxiety subsided, a feeling of intense happiness coursed through me, as when a strong medicine begins to take effect and one's pain vanishes: I had formed a resolution to abandon all attempts to go to sleep without seeing Mamma, had made up my mind to kiss her at all costs, even though this meant the certainty of being in disgrace with her for long afterwards—when she herself came up to bed. The calm which succeeded my anguish filled me with an extraordinary exhilaration. . . ."

Auguste Renoir, *Mme Charpentier and her Children*, 1878, Metropolitan Museum of Art, New York

This, for a kiss from his mother. Yet, as the reader, you feel—you are quite certain—that if only Marcel could get his kiss, he would live happily forever and ever. You believe this even though the book in your hand is heavy, and you know this will not be a short, lighthearted story. You never stop praying that the kiss will be the elixir that saves him.

Whatever your feelings about Renoir—and I for one detest his sweet, pliant girls, with their wan smiles and organza frocks—the mother in *Mme Charpentier and Her Children*, in the Metropolitan Museum in New York, is the Mother of all Mothers, the Ur-Mother. Surely I'm not the only one who wants to climb into that six-by-eight-foot picture. *Maman*—Mother—

spreads across the landscape of the painting. Her two children in their matching blue-and-white pinafores, the cozy black-and-white Newfoundland dog, the gilt furniture and lavish wall hangings, all breathe because of her. Her grace, her ease, her majesty. Her body. She is the warp and woof of this painting, of this life.

Colette is another great French writer whose mother, Sido, fills her work. Colette introduces *Break of Day* with a letter from Sido written to Colette's second husband, who has invited her to visit. "You ask me to come and spend a week with you," Sido writes, "which means I would be near my daughter, whom I adore. . . ." But Sido refuses: "The reason is that my pink cactus is probably going to flower. It's a very rare plant I've been given, and I'm told that in our climate it flowers only once every four years. Now I am already a very old woman. . . ." Then Colette's own text begins: "Whenever I feel myself inferior to everything about me, threatened by my own mediocrity, frightened by the discovery that a muscle is losing its strength, a desire its power . . . I can still hold up my head and say to myself: 'I am the daughter of the woman who wrote that letter. . . .'"

All day long French people touch, smell, eat, see, and hear what we Americans pay our psychiatrists lavishly to reconstruct for us: the love that enables us to create meaning out of the human condition, to either remember our mothers' physical and psychic generosity or make ourselves new mothers.

The rapport between French mothers and children can only startle an American. French women are affectionate but also demanding. They treat their children as responsible human beings who must be polite. They respect their children as individuals, separate and distinct from themselves. And mothers in France are people with their own appetites and eccentricities. They are never simply successful or failed mothers, accepted or rejected by their children.

Even their churches cheer the French on. France's great Gothic cathedrals are named for the Virgin Mary, the most sublime of all their mothers. Each is Notre Dame—Our Lady, Our Mother. In Amiens, Rouen, Chartres, Reims, and Paris. These are churches of unparalleled grandeur. Arcade upon arcade climb to vaulted ceilings. Arches stretch to consummate points, stained glass glows. Small intimate chapels circle the main altar, taking the visitor on a languid, twisty meander around the back of the church, accompanied by teams of sculptures and more colored, storytelling windows. The huge main hall, the nave and aisles—one or two depending on the size of the church—are adorned with sculpture atop columns, a rood screen surrounding the choir area worked up into the most intricate Gothic designs of figures and fruit and trees, animals, saints, and artisans. All this for Mary. In humility and grace, she who steps into the light. Not her son. You can't miss her. She is unforgettable.

In Paris's Notre Dame, Mary, majestically wrought in marble, lives on the right-hand side of the main altar. She is confident, lovely, purposeful. She sways there, hip shot forward, the baby Jesus held high. He's a little awkward, as usual too adult for a tot, but still cozily there upon his mother's body. They are so happy together. Who wouldn't long for such a wonderful mother?

This is not the bereft mother suffering at the foot of the cross. She is beautiful, graceful, captivating, and young. She is

Madonna and Child,
mid-fourteenth century,
Notre Dame, Paris

the Mary of the French heart. She is Mother, the source of all mothers, a piece of the mother-ballast from which leaps the serenity and genius of French life. I've walked across Paris many times to sit at Mary's hem.

You do find Mary in Italy, Spain, Ireland, and Latin America. But what you don't find is the reverberation through the culture of Mary-surrogates, guiltlessly taken into the mouth and soul. And with such pleasure.

Meanwhile, I've left my own mother in New York. I try to keep in touch, but I know it doesn't satisfy her, or me. She wants my body nearby, and I long for deep conversations with her. We are awkward with each other.

When my friend Chantal and I talk—when she recounts her memory of her mother pedaling her bike to a secret meeting during the German occupation, with three-year-old Chantal in a basket hung on the handlebars, papers hidden beneath her; or when we relish the pounding grace of Hemingway's prose together—she fixes me with her blue violet eyes that say, Try out something new on me, it will be fun. You won't fall off, don't worry. She's loving me in that moment as she has loved a child. And I do it, I trust her, and we dance like this together.

When my friend Muriel edits a manuscript I submit for her magazine, *Cause Célèbre,* she rewrites it smartly, teasing me on the way, her crystalline intelligence taking us exactly where she wants to go, but with wit and charm.

———

In France, a mother embodies the state as well as the church. Marianne, a sturdy peasant and the emblem of the French Republic, is depicted in thousands of paintings and statues, busts in town halls and postage stamps. She towers over Place de la République in Paris, large-hipped and large-breasted, wearing the Revolutionary Phrygian cap, her right hand raising an olive branch, her left resting on a large tablet on which is written "The Rights of Man." Robust and confident, she promises the French everything: Liberty, Equality, Fraternity, a country bursting with natural and cultural wealth. She is Renoir's *Madame Charpentier* as a peasant woman turned heroic, the young Virgin Mary as mature provider, a Mary who did not lose her son, a mother who never gave up a child.

Léopold Morice, Statue
of Marianne/la
République, ca. 1880,
Place de la République,
Paris

It is 2002, and I am on a routine visit to my doctor in Paris.
She looks at me and says, "You are a very sick woman,
Madame. You are losing a lot of blood internally. We must
get you to a hospital." I am amazed. I'm never sick. I'm like
my mother, a *starke*, strong. I turn to Ken, and I see that he's
scared. Usually when I look at him, I feel his confidence. But
now he can't help me, and it frightens him. I need a woman
today, a French-speaking woman. I need the absolute protection of a Mother who can communicate with the doctors
and take care of me.

I call Muriel. Though she is pregnant and preoccupied, I want her to be with me. I want her to be my French mother. In the emergency room she comforts me. I am trembling from head to foot. I'm sure I have cancer, that I am going to die, that I will have to say goodbye to Ken, that I'll never see him again.

My own mother wasn't reliable in tense situations. She was distracted and nervous, a party girl. Even now, at ninety, she's planning what she calls her last party, to say hello and good-bye to friends and acquaintances. She expects people as old as she is to hop on planes to New York to see her. Never mind their age; most of them can't afford the trip. She'll be surprised, I'm afraid, and I don't know how she will deal with the disappointment. But then, she has always taken in stride whatever comes her way. Maybe having kids was the hardest thing she ever did, and she couldn't say no to that. She had to do it, even though she was a working woman all her life.

I do not want my mother in the hospital. I want Muriel. After a few hours of testing and immense sympathy and delicacy on the part of doctors and nurses, it is discovered that I have a bleeding ulcer. The cause becomes obvious once I mention in passing that I quite love aspirins, an appetite I'd inherited from my father. For all my near-obsessive attention to health issues, I had been a blithe popper of aspirins all my life.

Some months later, when Muriel gives birth, Ken and I go to the maternity ward immediately. Never before have I understood how difficult it is to be a new parent. There are the two of them, Ed, twenty-eight, and Muriel, twenty-nine, and neither has the faintest idea what to do. Nor do I, of course. I, alas, am no French Mother for Muriel. Mothering is not something I ever strove for. I like to help other people, but the expectation that I will protect and always think first about another person and shape my whole life for them is not a demand I can satisfy. I know I would hurt a child. I would want her undivided attention and admiration. She would never be free of me. As I am not free of my mother.

———

Where but in France could Louis Malle's magnificent film of 1971 about mother-love, *Murmur of the Heart*, have been made? The early scenes take place in a spacious upscale house in Dijon where a happy, demonstrative family lives. There are two older sons, aged fifteen and seventeen. The youngest boy, fourteen, is the darling of the family. Between adolescence and manhood, he is amusing, sweet, and confused. The mother and sons cavort in a friendly and intimate way. Soon it is discovered that the youngest has a heart condition, the eponymous murmur of the heart. The doctors advise a health spa. The boy and his mother leave the city. Although the mother expects to have two suites at the hotel, only one is available. Their life grows closer. One day, when the mother is taking a bath, the boy peeks at her through the door. After she steps out of the tub and puts on her robe, she sees him and realizes what has happened. She slaps him. She regrets it, of course, and, while they are having breakfast, says "I should ask the manager for another room." "There aren't any," her son says.

A few days later, the boy knows his mother has gone to see her lover. He is disconsolate. When she returns distraught, she surprisingly tells him that her lover is moving to Paris and wants her to come, but that she cannot. He comforts her. "He didn't understand you," he says. "No," she responds. "But you loved him?" he asks. "Yes, of course," she answers.

Soon after, it is Bastille Day. There are parties all over the small spa town. Everyone dances and drinks too much. The mother falls into bed dead tired, saying, "I can't even undress." The boy says, "I'll help you." And so it begins, the scene of their lovemaking. Afterward, the mother says, "I don't want you to be unhappy, or ashamed, or to regret this. We'll remember it as a very beautiful and solemn moment that will never happen again. . . . It will be our secret. I will remember it without remorse, tenderly. Promise me you will do the same." He buries his head in her shoulder, and the scene ends.

How would my father have been different had he lived in a more sensual culture? What if he had spent more time savoring physical pleasures? He loved to swim, for example. And it was wonderful to watch him, those long, perfectly muscled limbs of his, his splendid head moving left and right with his breath, his arms neatly cutting into the water and out again. Forgetting everything. And oh, how he loved handball. Those aggressive slams against the court walls, not only to beat his opponent, but to make that delicious contact with the hard black ball and do with it exactly what he wanted. And then there was the dancing and the sunbathing. He enjoyed his body. But maybe not enough. Anxiety crept in fast. He never believed he deserved to be happy. And I suppose if he had led a more satisfied life, he and I would not have known each other the way we did. We might not have known each other at all.

Ken, on the other hand, expects pleasure and happiness always, and he gets it. People trust him and are nice to him. He, unlike my father, was lucky with his mother. He's made many paintings about her, although sometimes he doesn't even know he's painting her; he just draws a woman who happens to look like her. He writes texts in his paintings like "My mother had the sweet looks of an angel." Or "I'm six years old . . . I'm waiting at the kitchen table . . . she teaches us to make Hanukkah decorations with glitter and glue and colored cellophane. She used to be an Art Teacher. . . ." And when he turns to angels themselves, he worries. In his painting after the gorgeous Louvre Rembrandt angel seen from the back, Ken's text is "And what if you have a message to send back with the angel. A terrible tragedy is in the making! Can't you do something? What use is a divine messenger who will not deliver?" Deliver what? Or is it *deliver us?* From death? From losing the most bountiful love we'll ever have? All these paintings were for Ken's mother and for the love he looked for and mostly found all his life because she loved him.

⌒

People in France don't usually complain about their mothers. Only very occasionally does a rant erupt in a public forum, and invariably it sweeps in from the margins. In 1922, the

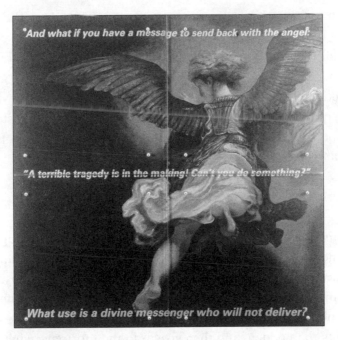

Ken Aptekar, *And what if you have a message,* 2000, Private Collection

German artist Max Ernst, working among the Surrealists in Paris, painted *The Virgin Spanking the Child Jesus Before Three Witnesses: André Breton, Paul Eluard, and the Artist.* A full-bosomed, large-hipped Mary flings a yelping Jesus across her lap and whacks him so hard that his halo falls off. André Breton liked the work so much that he reproduced it in the Surrealist movement's magazine, *La Révolution surréaliste,* in 1926. Leave it to the French to let a German artist travesty their most treasured totem.

Forty years later another outsider produced a mother-aberration. This time it was Louise Bourgeois, a French sculptor who moved to New York in 1938 when she was twenty-six and stayed there. In the 1990s she created life-size metal and wooden cells filled with repulsive-looking objects. They looked like uninviting "homes." Then she made giant, stalking, pregnant spiders. Sometimes a spider stands astride one of the cells. In 2000, a thirty-foot-high spider was installed in the Turbine Hall at the Tate Modern in London. It was titled *Maman*.

———

It turns out that if you do not love your mother enough in France, you can be severely punished for it. Albert Camus's character Meursault in *The Outsider* (*L'Étranger*) is a terrifying example. At the beginning of the book, Meursault arrives at the old-age home where his mother lived and has just died. He meets the warden, and then goes into the mortuary where his mother's coffin is set up on trestles. A caretaker offers to take the lid off the coffin. Meursault demurs. "No," he says. The caretaker sits down behind him. The two begin to chat. The caretaker is eager. He offers to get Meursault a coffee, and when he returns with it—a coffee with milk, a white coffee, an odd drink for a French person in the evening—Meursault decides he wants a cigarette, takes one out, and offers one to the caretaker, which he accepts.

A year later, when Meursault is being tried for a murder that occurred a week after his mother's death, he notes that the warden of the old-age home is called as a witness. He tells the court that "he'd been surprised by my calmness. . . . [He] then looked down at his boots and said that I hadn't wanted to see

Mother, I hadn't cried once and I'd left straight after the funeral without paying my respects at her grave."

Then the caretaker is questioned. Meursault observes, "He answered the questions that were put to him. He said that I hadn't wanted to see Mother, that I'd smoked, I'd slept, and I'd had some white coffee. And I felt something stirring up the whole room; for the first time I realized that I was guilty."

At the end of the afternoon Meursault's lawyer exclaims in exasperation, ". . . is he being accused of burying his mother or of killing a man?" Almost in response, the prosecutor leaps up exclaiming "I accuse this man of burying his mother like a heartless criminal." It is Meursault's behavior at the side of his dead mother that persuades the jury to condemn him to death by guillotine. Camus writes twice in the space of just two pages: "I hadn't wanted to see mother. . . ." The second time he adds, "I realized that I was guilty." He finds himself guilty. Never does he say to the court that the Arab he shot threatened him with a knife. Is *The Outsider* a new religious parable that tells of a man who does not sufficiently honor his mother and therefore must be put to death?

The Outsider is a stylish and morbid commentary on the French Mother romance. Camus, an Algerian-born Frenchman, a *pied noir*, as they were called, created in Meursault, also a *pied noir*, a man who, it can be construed, does not trust or love his Mother country. Meursault is accused of killing an Arab in cold blood, which he has not done, yet he passively accepts the indictment and the verdict. It's as if he understands and accepts that he is the Bad Mother that France became in Algeria to French and Arab alike, transforming them into murderers and victims. Not fifteen years after the book was published, France

embarked on a savage war against the independence movement in Algeria, which lasted eight years and which the French
lost. To date, neither country has recovered, not from the
butchery nor from the lies they told themselves and each other.
The recent French film *Caché* (Hidden) by the Austrian director
Michael Haneke—another outsider—reveals how the French
treatment of Algerians continues to mangle French and
Algerian hearts and lives in France.

—

I had a strange experience a couple of years ago at Christmas,
which fell at the same time as Hanukkah. One of my dearest,
most sensitive, most politically alert French friends came to
the house for dinner with a couple of small presents. One was a
candle in the shape of an angel, the other a sparkly glass globe
that would be most appropriate hanging on a Christmas tree.
Of course, she did not mean to offend me, but by taking *her*
Mother for mine, she made me invisible. And this friend of
mine is not religious; she is a secular French person.

And here we arrive at the dark side of French Mother glory.
That auspicious, generous, all-loving, and flirtatious Mother
is there for certain citizens, but not for all. French mater-
nalism is not proffered to nonwhite, non-Christian French
people, whether in the form of official state recognition of
their past and present—both as French person and immigrant—
or in the form of well-paid jobs or simple fair treatment.
These citizens are not on the receiving end of that nurturing
culture that breeds French self-confidence. Didn't the young
Muslims rioting in the suburbs in November 2005 feel like

motherless children, orphans, in that most maternal of countries?

We could say that French xenophobia is in part a desire to keep the French Mommy only for the French of European ancestry. That may be the danger of this Mommy-culture. It can drive you mad with possessiveness. She's *their* Mommy, not *yours*.

———

The confidence of the French is complete, the assurance of the beloved. Find a happy person and you will find a once-adored child. I've seen grown women, sophisticated French women, who, when they are totally at ease, stick their thumbs in their mouths and sit that way for long minutes at a time.

Those who despise the French detest their confidence, which they call arrogance. The French won't answer to anyone. They know what counts. I want what they have—the voluptuousness of their daily life, the rich complexity of their culture, their assurance. Their Mother. I only wish I felt as confident that Mother France wanted me.

CHAPTER 2

Tease

"She loves me, she loves me not." I peer into the heart of the French daisy, plucking out one petal after the other.

It hasn't always been this way. I had moments, even years, when France was the love of my life and perfect. That's how love starts, doesn't it? Before it dwindles to daily messiness and regressed emotions, before the wild rides and tender transparencies turn into old dungeons. Keep your lover at arm's length and you can prevent the descent. Temporarily. Keep him across an ocean (and preferably married to someone else), and your perfect love can last forever. That's how France and I stayed in love for thirty years.

I begin to get an inkling that all is not as I had thought with my faraway lover when, in the late 1980s, I have a startling encounter with some paintings. I develop a weakness for the French eighteenth-century artist François Boucher, he of the nymphs swimming alongside me in the New York pool. Boucher is not someone with whom I am meant to share an affinity. I'm a feminist and a social critic, and his paintings are all-girls and all-privilege, all the time. Fleshy, jolly, naked females on permanent vacation is not an obvious subject for me.

I know Boucher's paintings were made for the very rich. He worked for the Bourbon court, particularly for Madame de Pompadour, Louis XV's mistress. With the advantage of hindsight, everyone knows the price the French monarchy and nobility paid for their unearned wealth. The terrifyingly angled blade of the guillotine is there to remind us. Some would say—and I among them—that Boucher's paintings embody the insouciance of that court, and that one can see clearly in them—as in a crystal ball, really—why the French Revolution was on its way. Etched into their frivolity is stunning social inequality. But this, I am only half-ashamed to say, is not the trajectory that interests me.

It starts after I finish a book on Degas that was a study of his pictures of working women—laundresses, milliners, ballet dancers, and prostitutes. I admired his subjects and identified with them. They evoked pleasant memories of childhood outings, pretty hats picked out for the Easter Parade, clean linen flapping in the wind. And my mother, blouse pulled tight across her breasts, leaning into her iron, cigarette between her lips, happy. My Degas book loved women and the working class.

Like all my books, it had taken too long to complete, and in the end I am exhausted. But it's springtime in New York, and, with time on my hands, I take lazy walks across Central Park, often ending up at the Frick Collection on Fifth Avenue and Seventieth Street. The Frick is known for its French eighteenth-century rococo art—Fragonards and Bouchers, exquisite vases, tableware, and tapestried chairs. The coincidence of the American robber baron Henry Clay Frick collecting the finery of those other well-known champions of social justice, Louis XV and Louis XVI, is not lost on me.

No one I know at the time likes the rococo period, except Ken. All my art-historian friends are committed to the social history of art. We are analyzing Courbet's *Stonebreakers* and the peasant woman in his *Artist's Studio*, or Manet's bar girls and models. We look hard at how women were painted and ask, Why? One acerbic colleague writes a string of articles with titles like "Fallen Fathers" and "When Greatness is a Box of Wheaties." I am a little out of step, though, because I really like art, and many of my friends don't. They hate it. A French Marxist, the director of an extremely important art library in France, scrutinizes me one day, and practically yells, "I don't know why you care about Degas!" I am ashamed to tell him that I like the way his paintings look, and even more ashamed to say that I adore the fact that Degas painted and drew and sculpted working women. Smart and polite, this man, who becomes my friend, is also an ordinary sexist French Marxist: Don't talk to me about girls; first the revolution! I have to charm him, be feminine, make him want to help me. Which I do, and he does.

The Frick Collection is definitely the wrong place for me. I grew up in post–World War II America with an inherited disdain for wealth. Almost everyone where I lived on Gerard

Avenue in the Bronx was a socialist. It came with them from the Old Country, and they handed it right down to us, their kids. The worst thing you could do was cross a picket line. And you practically spit over your shoulder when you mentioned a rich person. Rockefeller, Ford, Carnegie—and Frick: They were all dirty capitalists. Wealth was evil, so how could you covet it? You wouldn't want to be Henry Clay Frick, would you? With those dead striking steelworkers on your hands?

So, what am I doing here? My dad's question again. Whatever it is, I'm enjoying myself. I wander the lavish rooms from Boucher to Fragonard and back again. I hear the slap of my shoes against parquet floors and inhale the smell of freshly waxed wood. Floating in this plush cocoon, returning day after day, it strikes me that I have enjoyed rococo art before, when I was a young graduate student in the 1960s. The professor who taught it was a sexy man in his mid-thirties who wore fitted Italian suits. He looked a little like my father, fine-boned, with a large nose, long-fingered, elegant hands, and a kind of prancing in his step.

While the rest of the faculty insisted on illustrating their lectures with black-and-white slides exclusively, considering them truer to the originals than the inaccurate technicolor ones, this man excited us with color. We might have whooped for joy had he not been so earnest. When he projected pictures by the seventeenth-century Italian artists Guido Reni and the Carraci brothers, in all their burnished, gold-drenched, and pastel hues, sighs did escape into the chandelier-hung oriental-carpeted room (with its floor-to-ceiling gilt-framed mirrors) that was our strange classroom.

But it was only when the Bouchers rolled across the screen that sparkles and smiles cascaded into the darkened room. Banished finally were the black-and-white bleeding Jesuses, weeping Marys, and risen Lazaruses. Here were delicious, round bodies in loveable pinks and purples, blues and yellows. Here were creased and folded textiles you longed to run your fingers through and thick, cozy spaces you could crawl into. Looking for all the world like cheap birthday cakes, they were paintings that no one should have liked—but I loved them at first sight.

Our professor spoke with a strange accent that I recognized as Bronx English, layered with English-English touched by Italian. Like me, he was trying to get out of the Bronx. He didn't know that he already had. Maybe you never know. Here he was teaching an elite subject—art history—at an elite institution— the Institute of Fine Arts of NYU. We were both there, he and I, and other "passing" Jews, infiltrating a Gentile field. I may have been the only person to wear jeans in that mansion on Fifth Avenue we called graduate school, but I was there climbing in the same upward direction he was.

Fresh out of New York's City College, with its great leftist history, I was suddenly lollygagging around in the eighteenth century. My Communist grandmother would have called it a *shande,* a Yiddish shame. But it was the 1960s, and, in retrospect, Boucher wasn't really that out of order. People were having awful lot of fun in his paintings, just as young people were all over our country.

In the late Eighties, however, when I am ambling across Central Park to the Frick, it is fifteen years into the women's movement and harder to rationalize these fleshpots of

François Boucher *Summer,* 1755, Frick Collection, New York

pleasure, where girls' bodies are common coin. Still, like Harry Potter, I crossed from here to Hogwarts and felt right at home.

The picture I linger in front of is Boucher's *Summer*. Three unapologetically full-bodied naked girls sit and lie amidst thick pink and amber, silver and purpley fabrics, leafy trees, and feathery shrubs. The sky's blue is as full of itself as the voluptuous girls in repose, the temperature perfect. Every form, color, and texture will always need and have its neighbor for company in this silken, safe never-never land. What a girl might find today in a spa, or a baby at its mother's breast. My own mother's body may have evoked no desire in me, but

Boucher's girls sing out Dylan's line loud and clear: "Come in," they say, "I'll give you shelter from the storm."

I take a long, deep dive into these unruffled summer days and linger where Boucher's girls lean into one another, and where velvety petals and tremulous buds ripple the paintings' surfaces. Even his male figures saunter and linger, as if their very masculinity has been leached out of them. Their bodies are dark, like the Egyptian or Mesopotamian males in tomb paintings, but nothing more distinctive than that. Themes of domination and submission are absent. They are not threatening. There is no place to triumph, no arena in which to show off. Nor are the boys less beautiful or less seductive than the girls. Everyone is content. Here is a utopian paradise, like a plentiful mother's body that will always say Yes to boy and girl alike, a land of pre-Oedipal pleasure where polymorphous perversity reigns and where male and female are not opposing categories. How I would have liked a life like that.

My friend Carol and I dance in the late mornings to Al Green. It's the 1980s and deep winter in Buffalo, where I'm visiting her. Snow pelts the house and weighs down the trees. Inside, steaming coffee and soft lights warm the gray day that is western New York winter. I've driven up from Binghamton, where I'm living temporarily and working on my Degas book. I've come for encouragement. Carol and I work and drink coffee all weekend. We go out for chicken wings. We dance. She always has a boyfriend. I'm hoping her desire will rub off on me. Habitually, I bury myself in my work, content but alone. I've had boyfriends, and even a husband when I was twenty, but there are long intervals in between. I don't really care except in the abstract: I should have a lover, shouldn't I? But the balancing act of work and love is not one I'm good at.

Ten years earlier, my father, visiting me when I was living with Carol, said to me, "What do you need a boyfriend for, darling? You earn a good living, you go to France whenever you want to, you have lovers, and, let's face it, you're smarter than most men."

He seemed happy enough to be my partner all those years ago when we devoured books together, swooned to Chopin, rushed and glided on the ice. Why didn't either of us suppose that could have been a model of love for me? Yes, sometimes it went a little haywire, particularly when I was young and I couldn't play the piano for him. I was an excellent pianist, but if he was in the room, my legs shook and my fingers turned to clay. A psychiatrist asked why I thought this happened. I murmured something like "He might have taken me to bed," and let the subject drop.

—

I once read a critic who described male desire as a rushing, antsy urge, a "pressing ever forward" that produces an "impatient economy aimed at [finishing]." That's not what you find in Boucher. Another critic wrote that because children are given their father's name, male eroticism is focused, "giving it the single goal of procreation." That's not relevant to Boucher's pictures either. No one is going anywhere in particular in his paintings. They dally, like Philippe and I did in our conversations and Ken and I do in front of paintings, at the table, elsewhere.

I'm flattered when my French dentist tells me, "I've never seen a mouth full of such even teeth in a woman, Madame. Only in men." When my psychoanalyst says he is concerned about my pronoun confusion, that I can't seem to get "he" and "she" straight when I recount my dreams, I'm proud of myself. I wish gender would go away. I don't see any fundamental differences between men and women, except that some have vaginas and others penises. What I see is society pushing us away from one other, naming us weak or strong, emotional or cerebral, poetic or scientific, passive or active, motherly or fatherly. Well, I am a strong, cerebral, active, and not-motherly person who happens to own a vagina. Of course my teeth are "masculine." It drives me wild when an American friend comes to Paris and buys her little girl a ballet tutu and her son a fencing mask and tells me later that she has no idea why he is so aggressive and she so sweet.

My father would certainly not have liked Boucher. Louis was good at certain pleasures—sexual and conversational—and not others. To him, control was most important; to Trudy, indulgence was. She was out of control. I wonder just how satisfying my father's sex life actually was, especially since his second wife said, "Poor Louis can't really have a sex life. His heart condition, you know." He didn't contradict her. Perhaps his silence was out of respect for his children, but I doubt it. I have a feeling that my father's game ended in denial and not the easy sexual pleasure his bravura publicized. How sad if that was the case.

As I linger at the Frick, deep in its hothouse garden and rococo plenty, the women's movement is beginning to fray. The certitudes produced by our first political realizations are breaking down, factions are splitting off to the right and left. The antipornography partisans are growing powerful at the same time as the idea of woman as earth goddess—all goodness and spirit—is gaining ground. How boring. We are back to "boys" and "girls" again. Good girls, bad boys. One feminist leader explains to me that she is so desperately trying to have a child because she misses the comfort and camaraderie of the old days. For my part, I'll take Boucher's bodyscapes, where males and females fall all over each other in an indeterminate heap of desiring flesh.

I want to chew and lick and wallow, far from rules and regulations, where boys don't get more than girls, where I can live eternally anchored in pleasures that never go away. What Proust's tall young milkmaid promises Marcel and what Degas's world of absorbed working women holds out to me. What fun it must have been to be a girl in Boucher's time! Yes, I actually make this irrational, uninformed, unintellectual leap, and I am so thrilled with my intuition about these paintings that I want to prove it. Wasn't it possible that far from leading inexorably to the Revolution, as I had previously thought, that Boucher's paintings pulled in another direction entirely, toward equality? I decide to try to find out if there's any truth at all to this hunch. I start in Versailles, the golden palace on a hill fifteen miles southwest of Paris.

Standing at the bottom of the road, looking up at the chateau, you feel as if you're entering another world, like when you tip your head skyward into a scene of serenading angels planted in cloudbanks high above the risen Christ in a Fra Angelico painting. At Versailles, no matter how old you are, you climb the cobblestones slowly, deliberately.

The day I take my mother there, years later, the climb is even slower. She might be any grand lady or working woman of today or yesterday, awed by the magnificence of French kings. But she's my mother, and I see her in her aged—if still sturdy—state. I watch her in all her eagerness and curiosity to see "how the other half" lived. "We going up there?" this eighty-five-year-old Bronxite demands in her booming voice. "Yup," I answer and look over at Ken: What could we have had in mind? We've already made her walk here from the railroad station. "You can do it, Mom," I tell her. She says nothing, but pitches her body forward for the climb.

The cobblestones are meant to be ridden across in clattering horse-drawn carriages, not stepped over by women in high heels or even in sneakers. It's a trek. At the top, I imagine the swish of satins on the ground as ladies step down out of their coaches. A necklace flashes here, an earring there, hats, feathers, and gloves, the rustle of fabrics one against the other, bodies already touching. Inside the palace, we walk through the sitting rooms covered with crimson brocade, one following the other, ablaze with chandeliers. I am regaled by the acres of walls and ceilings lined with paintings, the sweeping exterior views over fountains and gardens. Paintings of women in silk brocade and pearls, oriental rugs, gilt everything everywhere. My mother will love this as only a woman who has been a bookkeeper in the fur district all her life can.

She's no intellectual, my mom. In Hurleyville, she played cards with the girls. She smoked and kibitzed. She sat on the porch in her shorts and halter, her legs and arms and breasts all over the place. She and her girlfriends sometimes walked to town in the dark with only a few lights gleaming on the road. "Where're you going?" my grandma—Daddy's mother—demanded. "To town," my mother said. "Isn't it late?" "No," Mom said, looking a lot like a girl in a Boucher painting having her way.

Gazing out at the grounds of Versailles, I see a languorous parade of men and women in the distance. "We fashioned games of end-rhymes and poetic enigmas which filled the time," wrote Pierre Lenet in his memoirs, describing an afternoon at another chateau in an earlier period. "We would watch some of our number wander along the banks of the ponds, in the alleys of the garden or the park, on the terrace or across the lawn; alone or in groups, following the impulse of a moment; while others of us sang an air and recited verse, or read novels on a balcony, while strolling or while seated on the grass. Never has one seen such a beautiful place, in such a beautiful season, filled with better or more agreeable company. . . ."

Versailles is a history lesson in French pleasure. Today, anyone can have it, at least for a few hours. Class differences slip away. But that's not what Louis XIV had in mind when he moved into his grand palace, formerly a simple hunting lodge, in early May 1682. He meant to absorb aristocrats' attention in court homage and ritual and pleasure. And good manners. "He never chanced to say anything disobliging to anyone," wrote the Duc de Saint Simon, "and if he had to . . . reprimand or to correct them, which was very rare, he always did so with a more or less kindly air, hardly ever cuttingly, and never with anger. . . . Never was a man more naturally good-mannered . . . and so able to acknowledge age, merit, and rank. But especially with women, no one was his equal. He never passed the humblest coif without doffing his hat, and I am speaking of housemaids whom he knew to be such."

Pageantry dazzled the eye at Versailles, as banquets of unrivaled extravagance whetted and satisfied appetites. Conversation was cultivated as an art. Seduction would set the standard worldwide and, it would seem, forever. Most Americans think the French have better sex than we do, and all the time. And with strangers. In Bertolucci's *Last Tango in Paris*, Marlon Brando picks up gorgeous Maria Schneider under a railroad bridge in Paris. They spend days fucking in a once-glamorous, cavernously empty Paris apartment. In *Unfaithful*, Richard Gere—the darling-of-the-desired among American women (and men?)—could only sexually lose his wife to a charming and passionate young Frenchman, whom Gere has to kill to redeem his manhood.

The way the "masculine" figures, or does not, in Boucher's paintings starts at court. And it is the courtier that lingers in French men's bodies and self-regard today—the gesture of their hands, the lean of their bodies, the purse of their lips. It's what looks so feminine to Anglo-Saxon eyes, and is what my father meant when he said Philippe wasn't very masculine. Actually, my father's comportment and physique was very much like a French man's. As is my husband's, whose long, slim body is more giraffe than Marine. Men love him or hate him because there's no aggression in him. His body understands desire but not competition. Women are not sure about Ken. He's too nice, they think. But he's not.

———

Louis XIV "loved splendor, magnificence, and profusion," wrote the Duc de Saint Simon. "In the end he tried in this way to exhaust everyone by attaching honor to luxury. . . ." What an ingenious idea. Who but the French would think of it? Luxury, then, would not be superfluous or degenerate. Far from it. The more splendid, the more honorable. Like Abbot Suger in the Middle Ages, when he decided to decorate his church outside of Paris luxuriously in order to better honor God. He poured incense and wine into jeweled chalices, he threaded his robes with gold, he hastened the construction of stained-glass windows, and St. Denis, his church, became the first Gothic cathedral. Then Suger quarreled with Bernard de Clairvaux, who insisted on purity. He who was known for having ridden around Lake Geneva ignoring the sublime alpine views. Suger found ways to rationalize pleasure, and Suger triumphed, just as Louis XIV did, revolution or no revolution. Today the Eiffel Tower twinkles every hour on the hour, for the sheer splendor of it.

Ridicule was a developed skill at court, too. Brilliant nastiness could drive a person from Versailles, and even to suicide. A false step on the dance floor, laughing too loud or at your own jokes, flawed lineage, trying too hard, being too serious, all were reasons for the most humiliating disdain. A blade hidden in the satin cushions. How perfectly French that the cut of the knife is for judgment's sake. Just when you think you're home free, hidden in the curtained silky beds of Versailles and rococo opulence, servants at your beck and call, big black birds descend and carry you off. Like rococo pleasures, love can hypnotize you. You think you're safe, but one day you discover that you're not your old self, that your confidence is a puddle at your feet, and you hear your mother's mocking voice when your husband says: "Don't do that, I'll do it." "Is that the right address?" "Are you sure the plants need watering?"

———

Boucher, my painter of pleasure-for-everyone irrespective of their biological sex, made a lot of money from Louis XIV's great-grandson, Louis XV. He was Madame de Pompadour's favorite painter, and she was the most important patron of the arts from the late 1740s until her death in 1764. Boucher earned "50,000 livres per year," one historian wrote, while "an average comfortable *bourgeois*, living on revenues from bonds or real estate, earned 3,000–4,000 livres; the salary of a professor at the Sorbonne was about 1,900." Madame de Pompadour, a gourmet for all seasons and all senses, found her perfect painter in Boucher.

I had never given much thought to this woman. My art history professor treated her condescendingly. She was a spendthrift with indiscriminate collecting inclinations, he said. But now she looks like some kind of genius, the chief patron of this subversively egalitarian painter of endless Edens, in a world where if you were lucky and shrewd, you could have a very good time indeed. Even if you were a girl.

I have gotten carried away, I know. Of what importance could a girl possibly be in eighteenth-century Enlightenment France? But why not spin on the ice with my father drunk with desire and satisfaction both, and then go home and write an essay? Why not cozy up against my husband's back and then tell him I can't have breakfast with him because I want to work? What about desire and freedom? Even for a girl.

Born Jeanne-Antoinette Poisson in 1721 to a bourgeois family, Pompadour confided in Voltaire—whom Louis XV did not want at court, or even in France—that she "had always had a secret presentiment that she would be loved by the king. . . ." The story goes that her family encouraged her fantasies. The more connected to the monarchy these financiers and suppliers to the army were, the better it would be for business.

Pompadour was educated in the arts to a level that many bourgeois girls reached. She knew nothing about the classics or the sciences. Not long after she married, she either crossed paths with the king in the forest of Senart—where he often hunted, and not far from where she lived—*or*, and more likely, they met at a masked ball in the Hall of Mirrors at Versailles. It was 1745; she was twenty-four years old. He was thirty-five. In an etching of the event, he is dressed as a yew tree, she as a shepherdess.

It's a fairy tale, but Jeanne-Antoinette was not a girl who was going to live happily ever after. This story is Cinderella-in-reverse. Pompadour's real work began only *after* she met the king. How would she keep him? That is not the kind of pressure I would appreciate. But she more than managed. She

Interior of Mme de Pompadour's bedroom in her second-floor apartment, Versailles

surrounded herself with beauty and created it prodigiously—
that delicious rococo beauty.

Pompadour's rooms at Versailles connect by a hidden staircase to Louis's bedroom. They are bright, white spaces with
delicately carved wood paneling. Lush expanses of jade-
colored silk—Pompadour's signature color—fill the rooms, as
do porcelain, paintings, sculpture, rugs, and tapestries. Gilt-
framed mirrors and fresh flowers are everywhere. On the
mantel, a curving turquoise, white, and gold Sèvres clock bal-
ances on satyrs' hooves. Piled on top are rose blossoms.
Behind the clock, a mirror soars to the ceiling, held to the wall
by a finely carved gold frame riffing on botanical forms. Here
are marvelous nooks and crannies, textures and colors to
linger in. Just as the folds of Aldous Huxley's pant leg, in his
mescaline-soaked vision, taught him to revel in the hills and

valleys of baroque drapery, so I, in Pompadour's rooms amidst her pleasures, become lightheaded. The air trembles with promises. Forms, colors, textures pull me deep into my body, high into my senses, long into the layered knowledge that comes when sensual experience is transformed step by step, bit by bit, into the thickest emotional life. As it is too with the slow swelling of a Gothic arch, the rainbow hues humming in Cézanne's white tablecloths, the dark smells of French cheeses.

Ken works magic like this too. He furnished his tenement apartment, where he lived when we first met, with brass, velvet, porcelain, copper, and mahogany. He turned carved ducks, giant marbles, and anemones into theater on his simple kitchen table. He sewed a fire-engine-red silk scarf for me and talked me into buying a canary-yellow coat. When we married, he wore a white suit, his red hair glowing like the firmament in a Boucher painting. Indeed, Ken became a great fan of Madame de Pompadour and painted her likeness often, even obsessively. Across twelve portraits of her, he wrote phrases like "my dependence," "what I couldn't do," "my money worries," "the calculating careerist I wish I could be," "my beloved." One day he impersonated her—and Louis XV—in a video.

Boucher made many sumptuous portraits of Pompadour. One in particular is sheer sartorial delirium and measures about six and a half feet by five feet. The Marquise, as she is also known, is anchored in a sea of turquoise taffeta studded with pink roses and bundles of wide satin ribbons. She pokes her pink-shod feet out from under her petticoats. The fingers of one hand push into thick folds of fabric, the other presses open the

François Boucher, Portrait of Mme de Pompadour, 1756, Alte Pinakothek, Munich; © 2006 Marco Schuler and Ken Aptekar

pages of a book. Next to her is an inlaid table, its drawer pulled jauntily out, a key suggestively protruding from its lock. In the drawer, a white quill brushes against the table like a cat's haunches. Bunched-up drawings and scrolls of music lie nearby.

As much as I crave the fabrics, the mirror, the cushioned chair, I bridle at the parade of emblems, at what feels like an advertisement of Pompadour's abilities. Paintings with symbols are not unusual, of course. Sitters want to tell the world who they are. But the effort of the display, the fierceness with which Pompadour carves a place for herself at court, feels sad to me. It is this effort in all the portraits of her that renders her inaccessible and unknowable. She is not herself. She is a display of herself, and she is an offering to the king.

Who else could she have been, given the enormity of her desire and the normal restrictions on her sex? And I? Who would I have been? A clever Jewish girl living in a ghetto in Provence or Alsace, selling her father's wares on the streets, haggling, even as my father did for his parents during World War I? Or would I have dissimulated in Paris, where Jews didn't declare themselves until the Revolution? Or maybe I'd be a Jewish doctor's daughter, a merchant's daughter, a banker's daughter. A *tochter*. Always a daughter. What would it have been like with my father if I had been a boy? I wonder about that.

The dog at the left in Boucher's painting signifies Pompadour's fidelity to the king. She belonged to him. But surely that wasn't the whole story. She was a patron of the arts, a Medici, if on a philosophically more modest scale. She commissioned paintings, sculpture, music, prints, furniture, rugs, tapestry design, ceramics, and buildings. And she knew what power she had. "She looked me up and down with a haughtiness I shall remember all my life," wrote de Meinières, president of the French Academy. "Her head leaning on her shoulder . . . and sizing me up in a very imposing fashion. . . . I was as struck by her easy speech as by the perfection of the style . . . and I looked at her with pleasure and admiration. . . ."

Pompadour was a friend of Voltaire and a patron of Diderot's and d'Alembert's *Encyclopédie*—the multivolume encyclopedia that appeared between 1751 and 1772 and is among the most extraordinary products of the French Enlightenment. The political philosopher Montesquieu said, "In the eyes of postcrity, the representatives of the eighteenth century will be Voltaire and Madame de Pompadour." Voltaire wrote in a letter to Diderot that Pompadour was "one of us."

She was also despised. Louis's children called her *"Maman putain,"* Mother whore. The public mocked her and concocted nasty rhymes. They named them *Poissonades* after her maiden name, Poisson. Fish.

A small bourgeoise
Brought up in a bawdy way,
Measuring everything to the toise [a measurement]
Is making the Court into a slum. . . .

This inferior harlot
Governs with insolence
And it is she who awards
Honors for a small fortune. . . .

In the past, good taste
Came to us from Versailles.
Today, the rabble reigns
And holds the high ground.
If the Court is lowered
Why be surprised
Is it not from the market
That we get fish?

More recent writing about her is just as vulgar and reductive: "She exhausted herself in the service of this man . . ."; "The King still seemed infatuated . . ."; "Louis XV belonged to her.

She still intended to run his life down to the very last detail."
Pompadour "launched a charm offensive . . ."; "Whatever
Pompadour wanted, Pompadour got." Silly, sexist comments.
Only a few feminist historians credit Pompadour with intelli-
gence and discriminating taste.

How reviled she has been, yet what pleasure she created.
How many of those rococo delights would we have without
her? All those luscious Bouchers, gorgeous figurines, magnificent Sèvres tableware. Would we even know about Boucher?
If not, good riddance, according to my friends. But I don't feel
that way. I would have missed her and her legacy.

For five years, she had Louis's more or less undivided attention. She bought and furnished houses in the vicinity of Versailles that would please him, organized small dinners as well
as gambling parties, engineered theatrical and musical enter-
tainments in which she herself performed. Louis was a depres-
sive, melancholy man who did his best to keep ennui at arm's
length—"that anguished feeling of unreality and emptiness,"
one writer described, "that throughout the century would
threaten the euphoria of the privileged." Even kings. So much
time on their hands, so little to do.

Louis needed Pompadour. He needed the new bourgeoisie
she came from, that social milieu that knew so much better
than the aristocracy how to turn a profit from trade and then
from manufacturing. Louis required them in every aspect of
his life, including, obviously, his private life. You can be sure
that the cadence of Pompadour's language, as well as her ges-
tures and her tastes, were of a more down-to-earth nature than
his. So Louis flirted and bedded the very class that would
destroy him, that would remake France in the spirit of the

Industrial Revolution, liberal economic ideas, competition, individualism, and social responsibility. These ideas, and these people, would produce the untenable social and political disequilibrium that brought the Revolution crashing through the end of the century, a mere fifteen years after Louis's death. He had no idea of what was to come, but he experienced a *frisson* of a very particular order with Jeanne-Antoinette Poisson.

But, who was this woman? Perhaps there is more than a little truth in these words she wrote to her brother while she lived with the king, "I've seen so many things over the last four and a half years that I have been here, that I know more than a forty-year-old woman. . . ." She was twenty-eight at the time. A year later, she wrote to him, "Except for the happiness of being with the King . . . all the rest is a mere tissue of wickedness and platitudes, really all the wretchedness that human beings are capable of." And to a friend, "Alone, I try to forget the human race and distract myself with gardening. . . ."

What was it about Boucher that appealed to her? All those fleshy fantasies and rosy vistas, cupids, gods and goddesses falling over themselves gleefully, without sexual difference? There was nothing in her own life that resembled this. She was only the king's mistress. Only a woman. Always a woman. Needing a partner—this partner; subsumed in dependency as the self slips away. I'm sure she threw no tantrums when Louis spent the night with Mademoiselle O'Murphy and others. His distraction and self-absorption were normal. If he judged her, that was normal too. She willingly shaped herself to him. Did it give her sleepless nights because she wasn't writing, painting, composing, or executing scientific experiments? Why do I doubt it? Yet, even with the sweetest of men and centuries later, a girl will still immolate herself as she shapes her desires to her partner's.

So, Pompadour is a dead end. But I'm not ready to give up—not quite—so I think about the women who hosted the salons in Pompadour's time, the salonnières. Perhaps they were truer to what I see in Boucher's paintings. Surely they were different from Pompadour. At the very center of eighteenth-century intellectual and political life, they at least were not dependent on a single powerful man.

———

The salonnières, who all knew each other, managed sharp differences of opinion in their homes with grace and intelligence. They were people—Madames de Lambert, Tencin, Geoffrin, Necker, Deffand, Lespinasse—of refined literary and artistic tastes, and great shrewdness. Whatever differences politically and socially arose in their homes, everyone was treated with respect, and everyone who attended knew the rules.

Mme Marie-Thérèse Geoffrin was raised a religious girl and was married at fifteen to a man of forty-nine. At thirty, an experience at the salon of her neighbor, Mme Tencin, transformed her, and she realized her own curiosity and ambition. As one writer put it, though, her "ambition . . . would have gone nowhere without her entrepreneurial talent, her psychological intuition, and her ability to understand the times she lived in."

According to several witnesses, Geoffrin created the most stimulating and intellectually sophisticated salon of her day. Her guests included the writers Marivaux and Marmontel, the philosophers Montesquieu and Helvétius. She also was among the very few to invite artists, including Boucher, Hubert Robert, and the architect of the Pantheon, Soufflot. Like Pompadour, Geoffrin was not an aristocrat by birth.

Julie de Lespinasse, another salonnière, was a self-taught, down-to-earth woman who counted among her friends David Hume and the Marquis de Condorcet, as well as d'Alembert and the economist Jacques Turgot. At her death, she left 1500 pages of contemporary manuscripts and a cache of letters from Voltaire to d'Alembert and Condorcet and from Diderot, Rousseau, Marmontel, and Mme Geoffrin.

These are women who influenced public life. But much to my dismay, far from being welcomed and admired by most of their contemporaries, they, like Madame de Pompadour, were disliked. And despite the immense social and economic problems and inequalities of Old Regime France, many writers focused inordinate attention on the "woman problem."

Montesquieu, as early as 1721, bemoaned in *Persian Letters* that "these women [the salonnières] are all in touch with one another and compose a sort of commonwealth whose members are always busy giving each other mutual help and support. . . . It is like another state within the state, and a man who watches the actions of ministers, officials, or prelates at court, in Paris, or in the country, without knowing the women who rule them, is like a man who can see a machine in action but does not know what makes it work."

Montesquieu had more empathy for these women than his words suggest. He understood their desires as being simply human and expressed this understanding powerfully—also in *Persian Letters,* which ends with a declaration by Roxana, the favorite among the many wives of Usbek, one of the "Persian" travelers. She writes, "How could you have thought me credulous enough to imagine that I was in the world only in order to worship your caprices? that while you allowed yourself everything, you had the right to thwart all my desires? No: I may have lived in servitude, but I have always been free. I have amended your laws according to the laws of nature, and my mind has always remained independent." She then commits suicide.

Diderot worried that "too many women fall into gallantry—immoral lasciviousness. . . . No authority . . . holds them in thrall." He wrote in 1772 that "Woman has inside her an organ subject to terrible spasms, which rules her and rouses up in her phantoms of every sort. . . . All of her extraordinary ideas spring from this organ. . . ." The salonnières undoubtedly were not exempt.

Rousseau, haranguing courtly women, called love a dangerous "artificial sentiment which is extolled with much skill by women in order to establish their ascendancy and make dominant the sex that ought to obey." Rousseau, of course, is famous for his discourse on domesticating women. In *La Nouvelle Héloise*, he counseled French women persuasively—judging from the book's popularity—to be committed wives and mothers. And in a letter, he said: "Whatever she may do, one feels that in public she is not in her place, . . . everywhere . . . it is seen that, when they take on the masculine and firm assurance of the man and turn it into effrontery, they abase themselves by this odious imitation and dishonor both their sex and ours."

Why all this writing against desiring, ambitious women,

and by Enlightenment writers? Where is that seamless, unhierarchical pleasure of those bathing nymphs and cavorting gods, that pre-Oedipal playground of Boucher's paintings? What I have turned up is nothing remotely like a genderless utopia, an Eden of adult infancy where men and women are equal.

If the salonnières were so evident, and powerful, beyond their voluminous gowns and dining arrangements, why didn't they have more of an impact on other women and the writing about the sexes in general? Why did Rousseau's ideas about domesticity exert the greatest influence?

By 1793, in post-Revolutionary France, the *Journal des Révolutions de Paris* followed Rousseau's lead, advising its female readers to "be honest and hard-working daughters, chaste and tender wives, and wise mothers and you will be good patriots." A member of the General Council of the Paris Commune, addressing a group of politically active women, reproved them with, "Be a woman. . . . The tender cares owing to infancy, household details, the sweet anxieties of maternity, these are your labors." So pervasive were these ideas that when the militant Pauline Léon, leader of the Society for Revolutionary Republican Women Citizens, tried in 1794 to persuade the Committee of General Security to release her, she said, "I have entirely devoted my attention to my household and given proof of conjugal love and domestic virtues which are the basis of love for the country."

The Napoleonic Code, completed in 1804, was the deathblow

to any notion of women's independence. It includes, "A husband owes protection to his wife, a wife obedience to her husband"; "married women are incapable of making contracts"; "a wife may sue for divorce only in the case in which the husband introduces a permanent mistress into the family household." And so on. A gauge of Napoleon's "contempt for women," in the words of a prominent historian, is his attitude toward their education. "What we ask of education," Napoleon writes, "is not that girls should think, but that they should believe."

The salonnières were models for a different kind of behavior, emotionally and intellectually. But most women weren't interested. Hadn't there been any moment when self-determination was something women sought? Hadn't Boucher's paintings captured that ethos at all? The answer, I'm afraid, is a resounding No.

Despite complaints by some philosophers, women did not have any independent power. Madame de Pompadour might influence the king—and certain ministers—but she was totally dependent on him. The salonnières needed the presence of men to be who they were. They were hostesses. Informed and influential, but hostesses only. One rarely hears about a woman having affected anyone intellectually at a salon. Nor does one read of women participating as equals. Mme Geoffrin did not even take part in the salon discussions herself. Tact, apparently, was her strong suit. Her daughter said, "Fontenelle and Montesquieu praise her infinitely for that particular gift." Yes, well . . . tact. Women.

Lespinasse, at the beginning of her memoir, complained about being "educated above one's station." Yet she suffered from lack of confidence. One writer characterized her as having "a vocation for suffering." And recall that smart Roxana of the *Persian Letters* can only kill herself in the end. Montesquieu knew there was no place in the world for a woman with that confidence and those desires. He must have loved a few, though. At least one.

A recent historian puts it brutally and truly when he writes "The power of women in the eighteenth century is something of an optical illusion that magnified and made remarkable what was simply an aristocratic alternative to the dissipation of court life. . . . Madame de Lespinasse oversaw discussions of constitutional reform in the company of Turgot. . . . But is talking politics the same as politics itself?"

So, what are those Boucher paintings doing? Simply put, they are an intrinsic part of the vacuous, profligate life of the aristocracy. They may have heightened my own sense of the similarities between men and women and what pleasure could exist in a non-gendered world, but what has that to do with what they meant then? They are not signs of a subversive world of sexual egalitarianism; no such world existed. Nor are they part of the Enlightenment. What did they have to do with Montesquieu's *Spirit of the Laws*? That the law should be relevant to the people it governs, their work, the contexts of their lives, even the climate they live in? Nothing. Or with the *Encyclopédie*, which organized knowledge of all kinds accessibly so that it could be acquired through reading and reasoning by anyone who could read? Nothing. Or with the undermining of myth and superstition, in the interest of rationality and science? *Nothing.*

There it is. I was tricked. Or I tricked myself.

My friends were right, and I was wrong. Boucher's paintings *are* why the Revolution happened. Some say the rage of the peasantry toward the aristocracy turned the tide of the Revolution. Peasants bore the brunt of all the taxes, starved in the greatest numbers, fought in the wars. They were awed and enraged by the heredity rites of the aristocracy. How extraordinary that first statement of the *Declaration of Rights of Man and Citizens* must have been to a peasant: "Men are born and remain free and equal in rights. . . ." What glory in these words.

Given the state of the peasantry in eighteenth-century France, my dear Boucher uses them outrageously in his paintings. How can I now consider his *Springtime* at the Frick, where two so-called peasants flirt? These are not peasants, they are dolls—*poupées*—dressed in pseudo-peasant garb and set down in artificial landscapes. The leisure in the picture is aristocratic leisure. In any case, the very concept of leisure probably didn't exist then for a French peasant. It still doesn't. When Ken and I stayed in a bed-and-breakfast at a farm near Chartres recently, the farmer with whom we ate dinner became very exercised at the way most French people spend all their time planning vacations and not enough time working.

If there is no social or sexual tension in Boucher's paintings, it is because they carry the message they were paid to carry: everything is just fine the way it is, the aristocracy can have and keep it all. The ungendered "I" that I saw is not ungendered, because gender is irrelevant here. Class is relevant. The pictures are about the pleasures the privileged take because they *are* the privileged. The polymorphous perversity that so seduced me was the world of pleasure for the rich completely blind to the outside world. The calm in the Boucher paintings is their calm and confidence. They are the whole world, nothing else exists. I would not have existed. The sensual play grounds of those paintings was not for me, any more than Pompadour's satin dresses, flowers, figurines, and clocks would have been. Or the bon-bons, or the roasted pigs. None of it was for me. So much for the endless, "feminine," pre-Oedipal mother-love of Boucher's paintings.

And yet . . . and yet . . . didn't the French inherit something worthwhile from the eighteenth century? Voltaire, who would have known, wrote "Luxury is an extremely good thing." The *Encyclopédie* informs us that "luxe" can be "Lazy and frivolous" but that "polite luxury . . . always serves utility . . . [and] adds to the happiness of humanity." And Saint Simon's words, that Louis XIV attached "honor to luxury," describe much of French culture today. That is, luxury to the extent that a French person wants to create ease and plenitude in her home for her guests, for example. This is true even among poor people.

One night I am invited to a working-class suburb of Paris for supper. I take the graffiti-splattered elevator to the sixth floor, and, when I enter my friend's tiny apartment, she offers me champagne. A four-course dinner follows—including a cheese course—and coffee and cognac and chocolate afterward.

A middle-class friend will do it differently. He carefully figures out his guest list—which people will appreciate each other, but not too easily, not so that conversation won't become unruly and interesting. Then there's the menu to consider. Often there's entertainment, a trio of friends perhaps who play saxophone, drums, and guitar. Or new books and photographs to take down from shelves or out of portfolios, to be placed carefully in the hands of friends. Or a garden a couple of kilometers away that will offer the perfect after-lunch exercise and natural splendor for the senses. Once, an after-lunch gift is a trip twenty-five kilometers across the Spanish border to a bullfight.

One day, Chantal offers me a tour of her library, a white room with tall windows brimming with sunshine. She hands me beautiful editions of French, English, and American books, often paperbacks with Ernest Hemingway, Jean Cocteau, Marguerite Yourcenar peering from the covers.

Pleasure in perfect amounts and subtle varieties offered to friends. The host's honor *is* attached to this luxury, as one sense seamlessly meets the other, awakening the deepest knowledge and gratitude. I can't but think of Proust again, his mother's smell, the feel of the banister when he is sentenced to his bedroom, the teasing voices below, and later Vinteuil's sonata carrying lost love. The madeleine. But how did all the French get this way? So much so that when you receive a list of emergency numbers from your local seat of government, it includes *"coiffure à domicile."* Hair care in the home.

The eighteenth century is a large piece of the answer. So, obviously, is the Revolution, which took the privileges of the rich and spread them around. Which is what modern-day France in her economic policies still does, to the dismay of America and the rest of Europe. As a brilliant editor friend of mine put it recently, it is "not only the satisfactions of a French dinner party, but the French insistence upon certain entitlements in their everyday life, which create political realities unknown in America—the health care, daycare, superior education system; the short workweeks and long vacations that are about *egalité* as much as leisure and pleasure."

Eighteenth-century pleasures became the cornerstone of French life and French expectations. They are what we all admire, what we all want from our experience in France today.

~

One morning, I get an e-mail from our neighbor Isabelle. She's decided to stay in Nice an extra few days. How can she afford to go on vacation? I think to myself. She never has any money. My second thought is, *I* don't go on vacation! Of course I don't: I'm a Protestant American, even if I'm Jewish. I carry work madness in a gene.

I often watch Isabelle through my office window, sauntering through our courtyard. She is a darkly beautiful young woman with thick brown hair and a chiseled face. She falls in and out of love with other girls, and can be shattered by the end of love. But in the normal course of events, Isabelle packs herself off to the sea or the mountains for Christmas and Easter, long weekends, and at least a month in the summer. She always finds a friend or relative who has a house she can borrow, or at least a room with a view and undoubtedly a market teeming with succulent produce a few steps away.

I walk across to Ken's studio to tell him Isabelle's news. He looks up from his palette table and shrugs. "She knows how to live," he says.

We try to go on vacation. And we fail. One winter we decide: Enough is enough, we need a rest. We hear about the town of La Baule. There are health clubs and saunas there, masseurs, and a one-star restaurant. The restaurant cinches it. For three days, we wander around what turns out to be tacky La Baule, where sprawling, decrepit mansions advertise spa services that we never work up the courage to sample. Our room in the seaside hotel faces a pathetic patch of grass referred to in the hotel's literature as a garden. La Baule might have been Asbury Park, New Jersey, so international is its cotton-candy tawdriness and boardwalk lassitude. Day in and day out, we eat in the one-star restaurant, and even manage to get bored with that. We buy a white porcelain cow pitcher. At last, we go home.

Another great vacation of ours takes place the following winter. While our young and hardly flush friends, Muriel and Ed, leave Paris for Marrakech, Ken and I take a long train ride to gloomy Berlin of Nazi fame.

——

So, Boucher may have tricked me when it comes to equality between the sexes, but he didn't trick me about pleasure. And the Revolution made it available to everyone. Or did it? French people of Arab or African descent wouldn't agree. Nor would Jews have in the 1930s. The aristocracy before the Revolution felt that they *were* France, that *only* they were France. Outsiders—in those days peasants, artisans, workers, the petit bourgeoisie—were invisible. Outsiders are still invisible in France, and when they are not, they are shunned.

My father missed the Opera House in Riga when he emigrated to the U.S., but he did not miss the anti-Semitism. He was proud of the mixture of languages and cultures he grew up amidst, and he found that Americans didn't have that culture. Yet it is precisely that European culture that didn't want my father, and slaughtered the likes of him in the millions. How can one live with both feelings, loving a culture and knowing that it doesn't love you?

I drag an unwieldy bundle out of the eighteenth century. I'm not a forgiver. I don't let go of grudges. Neither the eighteenth century nor the Revolution treated women well, and the French Mommy Fraud continues. And yet, and yet. . . . The lessons of the body that are there for all of us, in themselves and as endless metaphor, flow right out of that century and into the best parts of our lives. The satisfying of Mother-longing that the French are so good at is good for me, too. I'm not willing to walk away from it.

CHAPTER 3

That Sunshine

You may love Impressionist paintings, I say to myself, but do they love you, sweetheart?

That may sound ridiculous, but when you spend a good part of your life with something or someone, it's the right question to ask, isn't it? I believe that depending on how a painting is made, it can inspire insight and deliver invitations, urge self-knowledge in all its many contradictions, make one wiser and kinder. I call that love.

The more questions a work poses, the better it is. I don't want sentimental evocations—of romance or family life, of peace and plenty, of complacency—from art. I want the hidden parts, the interstices, the chaos. And I want an adventure on the trip there. I want the surging pleasures, bright and dark, that come with revelation. This is what the French philosopher Emmanuel Levinas has in mind when he describes a shared conversation, two people, face-to-face, eye to eye, equals. That acceptance and respect. That is love, and I want that from art.

I have spent a lot of time with Impressionist paintings, and I do love them. I long for Renoir's bliss. I yearn to wander Monet's poppy fields. Degas's dancers puzzle me. I envy the dreaming French people lingering at riverbanks, waiting for that precious moment when they will fall in love and be happy. I have never known pictures that promise such pleasure and carry such fantasy. Everything will turn out well in this fresh, clean world where snow is pristine, and people ever young and happy. Even if as a kid I couldn't understand "young," I understood "happy."

And I am not alone in this attachment. Americans, who are not the most cultivated people in the world, recognize an Impressionist painting when they see one. And they enjoy it. The pictures tease contentment out of us, we who work so hard and who are so earnest, we who are known worldwide for our sincerity and punctuality, but not for our whimsy, not for our sensuality, certainly not for our long vacations. From childhood we know these pictures and taste their foreignness. They thrill us.

In the working-class Jewish neighborhood of my youth, we were edgy and bookish and not very athletic. Our families were, at most, high-school educated. Their first language was Yiddish. But even we, who are a notoriously verbal and not visual people, pinned reproductions of Impressionist pictures on our walls. Maybe we had some idea that they were European, from the Old Country, and so they vaguely resembled our family's past. Or maybe, to the contrary, they seemed entirely

American, like the word "fun." They're so fresh and optimistic, pretty and energetic.

One day, my mother and I pass a frame shop. I see her looking in the window at a picture of a ballet dancer. She hesitates for an instant, but then picks up her pace. All of a sudden she turns back and, clutching my tiny hand, enters the store. "How much is that picture?" she asks. She pays for it and tells me not to tell my father.

Now, it's one thing to buy an upright piano and fit it into the living room where my parents sleep and then find the money for piano lessons. That's expected. The children must learn how to play instruments. Piano for the girl, violin for the boy. But ballet? Who ever even *heard* of that? My father might talk with reverence about the Opera House in Riga, but I never heard anything about dancers. He boasted about the opera singers in his family. Every Jewish family I knew had an opera singer in the closet.

Over the years, my mother accumulated pictures of ballerinas, to whom she bears no physical resemblance, although she does love to dance and is great at it. She has gorgeous legs—gams, I heard men call them. Maybe she thought I could grow up to be like these dancers, or maybe the ballet was simply exotic to her and Gentile, a place where a girl could be perfect and American. I always thought of my mother as the American in the family.

Maybe you're surprised that a Jewish girl from the Bronx fell for landscapes. If so, you don't know about the Catskills and all the immigrant Jews who saved their money all year long so that they could take their kids a couple of hours north in summertime to "the country." It wasn't exactly rural. It was like the places Monet and his friends painted, little towns not far from the city. Our villages were called Loch Sheldrake, Hurleyville, Monticello, and Liberty; theirs were Chatou, Argenteuil, Trouville.

It was in those upstate New York towns that we jumped the barriers of city life and snuck into private pools and casinos, where we danced and gawked at older teenagers kissing and jitterbugging. We picked blueberries in sweltering afternoon heat, dropped them bursting into saucepans, and took them home, where our mothers piled on the sour cream, bananas, and sugar. We washed it all down with cool glasses of milk.

In the Bronx, the heat made the world dwindle and droop, but in the country the sun turned everything to its essence. It was in the Catskills that we learned to listen and to see, to smell and to taste. And to long for love. In my case, it was for blond waiters and my Pop.

It would be a late summer afternoon when my father came strolling up the road to his parents' house on one of his rare visits, arriving when I least expected him, a jacket thrown over one shoulder, his other hand swinging a small canvas bag. The late sun burnished him red and gold along his lean face and slender arms. His white, short-sleeved shirt opened wide at the throat, the pointy collar reached to his shoulder blades. His body hummed against the light cloth. He glanced this way and that, his nostrils flaring from the mountain smells; his ears pricked up to the sound of birds and to the clinking gas-station noises from across the road. He was confident and relaxed. Just like a young man in a Renoir painting.

Yes, we know Impressionism in America. Kids all over the country buy posters when they go away to school. The pictures make them dreamy, and within two years or three they pull on their backpacks and cross the ocean in search of all the pleasure the paintings dangle, but especially they go in search of love and sunshine. They go to Paris. No matter what the American government says about France, no matter how many Americans pour their French wine down the sewer or call McDonald's fat-soaked potatoes Freedom Fries, the kids—*and* their parents—keep coming to Paris to feel alive and optimistic. Americans have done so for a very long time.

Ben Franklin at seventy-seven came to raise money for *our* revolution and surprised his colleague, John Adams, by falling in love with several French women—who reciprocated his attentions. The artist Mary Cassatt wanted to deepen her knowledge about art (and we'll never know what else, since she saw to it that her letters were destroyed). Other artists who arrived were James Whistler, John Singer Sargent, Winslow Homer, and Thomas Eakins, and, later, Edward Hopper, Man Ray, and Ellsworth Kelly. Among the writers were Edith Wharton and Henry James, and, later, Gertrude Stein, Langston Hughes, Hemingway, Fitzgerald, Richard Wright, James Baldwin, Kay Boyle, Henry Miller, and Norman Mailer.

They came for culture. America wasn't supposed to have any. Henry James chided his writer friends for staying in the States. Go to Europe, he counseled over and over again. "Charming style and refined intentions are so poorly and meagerly served by our American atmosphere," said he. Others simply wanted to be away from home and came to France for the freedoms they'd heard about. All of them. Political, social,

Claude Monet, *The Magpie,* 1869, Musée d'Orsay, Paris

sexual. Many American GIs who stopped off in France during
two world wars stayed or returned afterward.

Impressionism for Americans carries the fantasy of that
large French life and those many liberties. Impressionist
painting *is* France to us. We want to believe in it and have it.

When I look at Monet's *Magpie,* I see Paradise. Snow-heavy
maples stretch and curl their arms around chopped, cold air.
Icy granules crunch underfoot. Wind whistles through the
fields. The speckled magpie regards his domain like a cock in
a farmyard, or like a girl holding her grandpa's hand as they
survey their little piece of land. Beyond the trees stands a

steep-roofed house with licks of brownish-red chimneys, and snow spreads across its roof like butter across bread. One imagines a house full of hearths and beds with downy quilts and feather pillows, a kitchen with copper pans, a woman cooking.

Who doesn't have fantasies about snowy scenes? There wouldn't be so many snow globes if there weren't so many dreamers. Sturdy country houses slumbering securely in white fields, the Statue of Liberty regal in the drifting snow, wise lions outside the New York Public Library wrapped in blankets of white velvet. All promise serenity for always. And Monet's winter landscape is not Dostoevsky's with his anguished Russian brooders and crazy families. No one will perish in Monet's snow, or kill anyone. The sun will protect you, promises will be kept, no one will be betrayed.

Renoir's subject is love, plain and simple. Straw boater hats dip and dive across his *Dance at the Moulin de la Galette*. So do the sighs and murmurs of the carefree young people. Men and women in a crush stand, flirt, and dance, pulled close or at a certain distance, which will shorten as the night wears on. Sunlight dapples the dance floor and bunches of white and brass gaslight fixtures wait to be turned on when the sun fades. Children with flowing golden hair are merry at the Moulin—"the mill"—too. Couples may hang on each other's arms, bending solicitously toward one another, but so do sisters and girlfriends, mothers and children. This is Renoir's magic at its very best.

The Moulin sat in what was still the no-man's-land of Montmartre, an undefined place between city and country. Working people of the neighborhood danced there on Sunday after-

Auguste Renoir, *Dance at the Moulin de la Galette*, 1876, Musée d'Orsay, Paris

noons. Two other mills stood nearby, and at one you could pay a tiny sum for a grand view of Paris. All that remains today are parts of a windmill situated next to an expensive apartment building, but many a tourist climbs winding rue Lepic in the 18th arrondissement to find the mill, so much do they desire what is in Renoir's picture.

My mother was a poster girl for pleasure, a brunette Marilyn Monroe. She was up for anything. She was our American. Wanna go to a nightclub? Yes. Dancing? You bet. Out to eat? Absolutely. She wasn't going to stay home and brood, going around and around about why Louis had girlfriends. She was going to find a Renoir painting to jump into.

Does it matter that Renoir was a vulgar man who said things about women like, "She even makes mistakes in spelling, and in my opinion that's essential to a woman"? Or, about a woman lawyer, "I can't see myself getting into bed with a lawyer. I like women best when they don't know how to read; and when they wipe their baby's behind themselves." He was even worse on Jews.

John Berger, the English critic and novelist, once showed a picture of wheat fields by van Gogh on one side of a page in a book, and when you turned the page you saw the same picture with hand-written words beneath telling you it was the painting van Gogh was working on when he shot himself. The painting will never look the same. Nor do Renoir's paintings to me, after I read his words.

———

There is no great museum in America that doesn't have its cache of Impressionists—Boston, Chicago, Cleveland, Kansas City, New York, Philadelphia, Washington. We are the greatest collectors of these paintings in the world. We could have looked elsewhere for our sunshine and landscapes. In Italy, for example, there were the Macchiaioli, nineteenth-century artists like Giuseppe Abati, Giovanni Fattori, Vito d'Ancona, Silvestro Lega, all of whom painted intimate canvases of sun-baked landscapes with stucco houses and river banks, horses pulling carriages along dusty roads, shaded interiors with mothers and children, all painted in vivid blotches of saturated color. These paintings never appealed to Americans. And then there is German Romantic landscape painting, most famously by Caspar David Friedrich, whose icy vistas, craggy cliffs, and solitary figures staring out to sea never captured our imaginations either. We Americans are simply unreconstructed—if very embattled—Francophiles.

We may think to ourselves, "These French people don't work very much, do they?" "They're not that clean, either." "They're arrogant and conceited, and they don't really like us." Nevertheless, we can't stop visiting their country, fantasizing about lingering in cafés, strolling the narrow streets of the Latin Quarter, falling in perfect love. No foreign country is written about more by our press than France. I may have come to her across Eastern Europe with my father, but Americans arrive from all over, pulled across the ocean by longing. Impressionism and the Eiffel Tower are the bait.

We weren't born loving Impressionist painting, of course. For one thing, we simply don't see German or Italian pictures in our museums, unless we go foraging. So how could we possibly like them? But its appeal goes beyond familiarity. Impressionism, on the other hand, is everywhere. This French painting embodies our fantasies in ways Italian and German culture do not. We are supposed to be a fun-loving, beer-slogging, "hail fellow, well met" sort of people. We are also considered vulgar and uncultivated, and we know it. Our current president, George W. Bush, curries favor as well as votes by cultivating precisely this image. But many Americans are ashamed of this cultural lack, and France is the country of ultimate savoir faire. We turn to her with envy mixed with shame, to learn about pleasure and loftier notions of happiness.

Perhaps it's also true that we don't have as much fun as we'd like to, and that we reach for Impressionism because we desperately want to enjoy ourselves. Perhaps the paintings represent not who we are, but who we'd like to be.

Americans started buying Impressionist canvases almost as fast as they were made. We own more works than the French do. Mary Cassatt, a close friend of Degas, brought her friend Louisine Elder (later Havemeyer) into the Paris art world in the mid-1870s. Cassatt was thirty when she met Louisine, an adoring nineteen-year-old, who later wrote of her friend, "I felt then that Miss Cassatt was the most intelligent woman I had ever met, and I cherished every word she uttered, and remembered almost every remark she made. It seemed to me no one could see art more understandingly, feel it more deeply or express themselves more clearly than she did."

We Americans have a lot to thank Miss Cassatt for, too. The magnificent Havemeyer collection lies at the heart of the Metropolitan Museum's Impressionist holdings in New York.

Because rich people talk to each other and imitate each other, in the early twentieth century, the Ryersons, Potter Palmers, and Coburns in Chicago began purchasing these paintings in quantity. In 1886, the shrewd French art dealer Paul Durand-Ruel, during an economic slump in France, went to New York with more than three hundred Impressionist paintings. He had great success there, and in effect opened the American market to Impressionism.

It is tempting to think that all those American millionaires, driven by their Protestant work ethic, fell in love with Impressionism precisely because they weren't having enough fun by far, or perhaps because they knew that, in their reveling, their souls remained virgin.

———

I'm twenty-one, and early on Saturday mornings, while my husband sleeps, I take the M4 bus from Washington Heights down to the Metropolitan Museum of Art. I climb the large central marble staircase and head toward Degas's *A Woman Seated Beside a Vase of Flowers*. I nod to the guard and sit down on the bench in front of the large two-and-a-half-by-three-foot painting. Filling two thirds of the canvas, white, pink, purple, yellow, and burgundy-colored asters push, fall, and nod in a round, fluted glass bowl. Next to them sits a woman dressed in mauve. Pushed into the right side of the picture, she leans pensively on the table, her fingers touching her cheek and lips. She stares into the distance. So penetrating is her gaze and so particular her carriage that she takes up as much emotional space as the flowers.

Impressionism starts for me as an adult with this not very Impressionistic portrait, a woman marked by her intelligence and solitude, a woman waiting. She holds her own against the flowers, but only just. She is stubbornly drab. Something is wrong with her. She's afraid. She peeks at desire during an opera or on the pages of a novel. Then she pretends indifference. She will live and die never knowing love. Maybe she asks, as Ken does later in a painting he makes, "Why can't the people you love live forever?" Maybe that's why she can't fall in love. She knows it will end one way or another, and she can't bear the thought of it.

⁓

Near the middle of the twentieth century, a curious thing happens to Impressionism. A brilliant art historian named Meyer Schapiro makes it his subject. This is strange, because

Edgar Degas, *A Woman Seated Beside a Vase of Flowers*, 1865, Metropolitan Museum of Art, New York

Modern Art, which at that point starts with Impressionism, is off-limits as a field of study. Scholars say you can't have a critical distance from art that was made so recently. Schapiro wrote his dissertation at Columbia on French Romanesque sculpture. An odd subject for a Jew, you might think, but not at all. It is exactly the type of subject one worked on if one wanted to succeed in this world. There weren't many Jews in art history at the time. Schapiro's teachers' names were William Bell Dinsmoor, Ernest DeWald, Charles Rufus Morey, and Marion Lawrence.

I don't know what brought Schapiro to Impressionism, and

Ken Aptekar, *Why can't the people you love live forever*, 1999, Private Collection

no one who knew him, and who is still around, can say. Perhaps it was what brought me. The fun of the paintings, and how American they are by sheer association with all those museums and galleries that hang them and street vendors who hawk them. These pictures carry no hint of Brownsville, Brooklyn, where Schapiro came from, or the Bronx. There is nothing Jewish about them. Though it turns out you can make them Jewish.

"Foreignness" was Schapiro's milieu. He grew up hearing Yiddish, German, Russian, and English. Socialism was also home to him. People often say that when Jews became secular after the Enlightenment, they moved steadily leftward, and Marx took the place of God. Or, at least, socialism did. By the 1930s, Schapiro was a politically engaged leftist and part of a group that came to be known as the New York Intellectuals and included Paul Goodman, Philip Rahv, Harold Rosenberg, and Sidney Hook.

Shapiro wrote about Impressionism for the first time in 1937, which as it happens was right in the middle of the Spanish Civil War, a conflict that mesmerized the American Left. The late Thirties was also when the extreme Left and the Center Left unified in the States and France into what became known as the Popular Front, but which just a couple of years later would be crushed in Europe by French and German fascism. Obviously, the radiance of Impressionist painting was a far cry from the storms blowing across Europe, but Schapiro was never one to focus on pleasure. It didn't figure in his critical apparatus. On the contrary, he set in motion a critical view of the paintings that is Talmudic, so riddled with questions did those sparkling landscapes become. Since Schapiro, Impressionism has never been the same.

For him, the people who enjoyed the paintings in the nineteenth century had the time and means to relish sensation, not as it was experienced in daily life, but as it was proposed to them in a work of art. They—the enlightened middle class—had the freedom to experience their senses because their lives weren't completely absorbed by earning a living. He writes, "It is remarkable how many pictures we have in early Impressionism of informal and spontaneous sociability, of breakfasts, picnics, promenades, boating trips, holidays and vacation travel. These urban idylls not only present the objective forms of bourgeois recreation in the 1860s and 1870s; they also reflect in the very choice of subjects and in the new aesthetic devices the conception of art as solely a field of individual enjoyment . . . and they presuppose the cultivation of these pleasures as the highest field of freedom for an enlightened bourgeois. . . ." To a social critic like Schapiro, it went without saying that this class of people were benefiting from the poorly compensated labor of others. Schapiro was trying to figure out what that pleasure-seeking meant to a nineteenth-century viewer, to the artists who created it, and perhaps to himself as well.

It is, it seems, the destiny of those joyous paintings to attract leftist critics who can't let them be. I'm afraid I include myself here. Rather than abandoning ourselves to their evident attractions, we are haunted by Walter Benjamin's disturbing words, written in 1940 when he was fleeing the Nazis. For the critical leftist, he wrote, all great works of art "have an origin which he cannot contemplate without horror. They owe their existence not only to the efforts of the great minds and talents who have created them, but also the anonymous toil of their contemporaries. There is no document of civilization which is not at the same time a document of barbarism." What a terrible burden for art to bear, and for us viewers as well. So, you see, we made Impressionist paintings just a little bit Jewish.

I liked the fact that Schapiro was a Jew who spoke with a heavy Brooklyn accent and penetrated the Gentile world of art history. He was inspired in his writing about Christian art, *and* he thumbed his nose at that world by writing about something else entirely. Schapiro could be a Jew, an outsider, but also an insider. He could be an American. But he wasn't "passing." He was actually both.

My father always said, "Stay away from Gentiles." Ruthlessly he laced into the great love of my brother's life when, in his mid-twenties, he decided to marry. "She's fat," my father wrote to his son. What he was really saying was "She's Gentile and stupid." At that time, this particular stupid Gentile was on her way to becoming a brilliant lawyer. My father had no idea how anxious and angry Gentiles made him, how miserable and deflated he became in their presence. How afraid he was of them. In a split second of psychic displacement, he turned his miseries into judgment. He never removed this armor.

Jewish intellectuals like Schapiro helped make it possible for Jews to think about Gentiles and Gentile culture in a new way, to throw our worries about inferiority, our fear of death and betrayal, into the way we look at and write about culture. The urge to endlessly question came right up out of our historic legacy.

Schapiro's Impressionism was Parisian scenes of pleasure, mine was *A Woman Seated Beside a Vase of Flowers,* a picture of a reticent woman lost in thought. When I was little, my father held me on his lap facing him and wrinkled his brow. Up and down, up and down it went, and he said, "Now you do it, Eunie." He was teaching me to worry. I grew up longing to dance at the Moulin de la Galette, to be chosen by a gallant young man, to wear crinolines and frills, to be happy. Instead, I became a worrier.

My mother waited for Valentine's Day cards, and what she got was my father, Mr. Devil-May-Care-Dandy, who could have stepped right out of a Renoir painting, but not toward her. That was my father's trick. He'd get you going, and then leave. He made me furious when, years later, after their divorce, he asked, "How's Mommy doing?" "All right," I muttered. But I wanted to scream, "Shut up, will you? You don't give a damn how she's doing. You just want to hear that she still loves you, that she'll never love anyone but you. Okay, here it is, Pop: She'll suffer through eternity because she loves you so much. Happy?" My mother fooled us all, though, and when my father died thirty years after their divorce, it was obvious that she was relieved.

Carol and I, graduate students at Columbia and NYU respectively, are sitting one early July evening in the garden of the Museum of Modern Art. The larger-than-life-size bronze sculpture of a washerwoman by Renoir faces us. Until that day, I hadn't realized how much I hated that sculpture. I feel like a voyeur looking at this woman on all fours, washing clothes. Why is she performing this intimate chore here in full view of urban passersby? She belongs in the country on the banks of a river, or in a communal town laundry where she is with other women doing the same job. You don't watch somebody washing clothes any more than you watch someone cleaning your house. It's not polite. The sculpture's bronze material itself denies that anything remotely like what is being represented is happening. This exhausting job—and who can imagine a man on all fours doing the same thing in a sculpture?—is transformed by the bronze into something heroic, even religious, when it is just hard, ordinary, female work. It's a lie from start to finish, and it irritates me. Carol meanwhile continues sunning herself and chuckles at how irate I've become.

It might have been that day that I took a longer look at Degas's ironer, just up Fifth Avenue at the Met. I love the concentration and chatting that can accompany ironing, the spritzing of the water, the starched new linen. My mother and I spent some sweet moments together while she ironed. Carol and me, too. But in his painting, Degas is not representing the woman in his life ironing, for two simple reasons: First, there was no woman in his life; and second, even if there had been, she would not have done her own ironing. Degas is painting a professional ironer—who, unlike Renoir's scrubbing laundress, you would have been able to see in the middle of a city. They were everywhere in the late nineteenth century—in their ground-floor shops, or traipsing the streets, their large baskets at their hips. Through open windows or doorways, you would have glimpsed women pressing into their irons or holding them up to their faces to test the heat. Sometimes you might catch them drinking wine, or sprinkling water on sheets and blouses.

Zola writes in his novel *L'Assommoir* that the laundress Gervaise "enjoyed putting her iron down for a minute and going out to the doorway to beam at the street at large. . . . Standing there in her white bodice, bare-armed and with her fair hair blowing loose from the flurry of work. . . ." Gervaise's neighbors stop by. In winter, her laundry shop is "a haven of refuge for all the chilly people in the neighborhood . . . it was nice and warm there. There were always chattering women having a nice warmup by the stove. . . ."

What I see when I look at Degas's ironer at the Met that day is a sun-drenched room smelling of bleached linen. Nostalgia washes over me. Like Renoir's sculpture, the ironer also resides in a happy, sun-drenched world, where even back-breaking work is pretty. But the more I look at this ironer, the more I notice that something else is taking place. A hint of another, more troubling experience hides just behind the sun-shine, and it gives me a start. It is as if something I've always taken for granted is not exactly what I thought it was—like when a woman living all her life with a companionable hus-band discovers after thirty years that he's been involved with another woman all those years.

At about the same time, Renoir's pictures begin to irritate me. They are too happy. They're *obsessively* happy, it now seems. It is the late Sixties, the beginning of the women's movement, and perhaps it's obvious to me that I could never be a girl in his paintings. Even the Monets, Sisleys, Pissarros, and Morisots begin to appear relentless in their optimism. I loved—do love—them for that, but it reminds me of the pressure I often experi-ence when men ask me why I don't smile more. Perhaps I never trusted the truth of the paintings, any more than I did the Par-adise of Hurleyville. At least Proust lets you know that perfect love is unattainable. That you may glimpse it as it rushes by, but that, when it makes a stop in your life, you see what a miserable thing it is. You see that it doesn't last. Renoir's pictures look more and more like Snow White, Cinderella, and Rapunzel all wrapped up in one. That's what I knew then, in the late Sixties. I got divorced in 1967, two years after my parents did.

When my father visited us in Hurleyville, after months of being away, I waited for him at the gate, and I worried if I looked nice.

"Daddy!" I cried out when I saw him.

"Eunie, *Meydele,* how is my *sheyne?* Look how nice and thin you look. What pretty shorts."

"I'm fine, Daddy. I'm so glad you're here. How long are you staying?"

"I haven't been keeping you waiting, darling, have I?"

"No, Daddy," I lied. "I was reading."

Later we sprawled in the backyard together, he in a metal lawn chair, I on the grass. He didn't like to muss his clothes. He took off his shirt and folded it neatly. His face and chest turned to the sun like a flower. He closed his eyes and sighed. I tried to sit quietly as I waited for him. Ten minutes later, he'd smile and ask me a few questions about what I'd been doing. When I tell him, his eyes glaze over. Soon he says he'll take a walk to town and doesn't invite me. Wouldn't he like to amble the road with me and hold my hand, I wonder, like Grandpa and I do? Then the sunshine would go on and on and my father and I could be happy together always.

One can say that eighteenth-century art is exuberant and optimistic, and I started my last chapter saying precisely that. You don't have to think too hard, though, to imagine the squalor on which the insouciance of these paintings rests. You look at them and you know exactly what Walter Benjamin was talking about. But Boucher never pretended to realism. He was painting a gilded sliver of society. The Impressionists, on the other hand, do promise real life, and a great life at that. But it is a false promise. I may have had my private and political reasons for becoming uneasy about these paintings, but there is also a certain disingenuousness embedded in them as well.

If Impressionist paintings observe nature in detail, as in the flicker of sunlight on water or on leaves, or on a girl's face, they ignore the larger picture. What they paint is a small piece of the truth, but they do it with such élan, and so completely, that we never think about what's not there. In a Vermeer, you might wonder what's outside the window, in a Constable where the wagon is heading, but in a Monet, the sunlight becomes your whole world. As Cézanne said of Monet, "He is just an eye. But what an eye."

Impressionism seems to stand outside of history. Art in general does for most people, but Impressionism most of all. In part, it is the prosaicism of the subject matter. There is no classical or religious symbolism to decipher, there are no historical narratives to untangle, no unwieldy emotions to sort. When one looks at Botticelli's *Birth of Venus,* one considers the Renaissance in Italy. A Rembrandt portrait brings seventeenth-century Holland to mind. But Impressionism suggests nothing but itself. And though the paintings are 120 years old, they read as now. The sunnyness is France, pure and simple. That sunshine.

But it isn't. Just consider Paris weather. The French capital is as perennially gray and rainy as London. Where is that grayness in the paintings? Now, it's true that Paris does have sunny days, and they are glorious. So it's not as if depicting Paris in the sun is not true. But to paint *only* sunny days, again and again and again, was, well, compulsive. The myth of sunny Paris is mighty, and Impressionism has contributed mightily to it.

In fact, those glorious, carefree paintings tiptoe around the disturbing circumstances that produced them. The 1860s to the mid-1880s—the period of Impressionism—were not years of prosperity and security in France, they were not sunny years. Much of Paris was torn down and then rebuilt) by Baron Haussmann at the behest of the French ruler, Napoleon III; industrialization was reshaping the face of economic and social life; France was humiliatingly defeated in a war with Germany in 1870; a vicious insurrection—a civil war, really— erupted in the same year in Paris; and an economic depression devastated the country.

Between 1852 and 1870, Haussmann plowed boulevards north and south, east and west, connecting railroad stations and creating greater mobility. The total length of sidewalks in Paris increased from 155 to 683 miles. About thirty-four thousand new buildings were added, many with the now-signature wrought-iron balconies facing the spectacle of the city. The new boulevards were perfect for café terraces and strolling, but also for aiming cannon.

Haussmann built, and he destroyed. He cleared ghettos and moved the poor to the fringes of the city. A catalyst for the entire rebuilding project was to get the "dangerous" class (the poor), who were perceived as politically provocative, out of the center of town. From 1789 to 1848, the people of Paris erupted in revolution three times. Much to the dismay of Haussmann and

Louis-Napoleon, revolution blew up again in 1870, after their rebuilding project.

But in the long run, Haussmann succeeded wildly. France today has inner cities that are largely white and middle-class, and suburbs—or *banlieues,* as they are called—that are primarily inhabited by descendants of Arab North Africans and recent sub-Saharan African immigrants. The so-called dangerous classes are in exile outside of the city, where they are now becoming truly dangerous and for good reason. They are the new century's *enragé,* the roaringly angry. Where, they wonder, is French liberty, equality, fraternity? They were lied to—just like the picture-postcard Paris that we all love lies to us about the city's population and its malaise. And just like Impressionism shied away from the bleak, the dirty, or the anxious.

Obviously, we all see things differently, but what we see and what we tell is a choice, and significant for that. The Goncourt brothers, two writers and contemporaries of the Impressionists, wrote on November 18, 1860: "Our Paris, the Paris where we were born is passing away. . . . Social life is going through a great evolution. . . . I see women, children, households, families in this café. The [home] interior is passing away. . . . The club for those on high, the café for those below. . . ." The brothers were inconsolable.

The great poet Charles Baudelaire, however, was enchanted by the new city. In 1863, he wrote about the dandy, the *flaneur,* saying that "The crowd is his domain, just as the air is the bird's. . . . His passion and his profession is to merge with the crowd . . . it becomes an immense source of enjoyment to establish his dwelling in the throng, in the ebb and flow, the bustle, the fleeting and the infinite." At every step, a discovery.

In Zola's 1883 novel *Ladies' Delight*, a book about the department store Bon Marché, two salesmen whisper to each other about a customer. One says: "A tart? No, she looks much too genteel. . . . I should think she must be the wife of a stockbroker or a doctor, well, I don't know, something in that line." And the other replies: "Oh, go on! She's a tart. . . . It's impossible to tell nowadays, they all have the airs of refined ladies."

Artisanal jobs like shoemaking, ceramic production, and weaving were industrialized, and people lost the sense of accomplishment that comes with creating something from start to finish. They could only sell their labor, not the goods they labored over. A hole was hollowed out where confidence and conviviality had been. Alienation swam in, with its partner anxiety. Fewer people turned to priests or God for help.

Women entered the work life of Paris as clerks and salesgirls, factory and sweatshop workers. Stylish clothing became cheaper to buy, due to machine manufacturing. All the girls and women looked charming. They strolled with each other or with men. Sometimes alone. Mary Cassatt went out to the Louvre or to buy art supplies, to the theater, or to socialize with French and American friends. Usually she was with her sister or mother. Occasionally she was alone. The English artist George Moore, a friend of the Impressionists and an habitué of their favorite café, the *Nouvelles Athènes* at Place Pigalle, said Cassatt "did not come [to the café], it is true, but . . . we used to see her every day." And, as one Cassatt authority suggests, they might have run out to chat with her as she walked by on her way to her studio.

Berthe Morisot, similarly wealthy and a working artist, led a more sheltered—perhaps a more French—life, but one hears of her dining at the Manets'—she ultimately married Manet's brother, Eugène—and attending the annual painting salons.

Victorine Meurent, a working-class woman, walked the city as she pleased. She was a professional model. Manet's most daring paintings are of her, including *Olympia* and the *Déjeuner sur l'herbe*. Meurent, miraculously, was also a painter. Since making art is a middle-class profession, I always wondered how she imagined herself out of one class and into another, that old, intriguing question of how desire comes to life in a person. In any case, she didn't need the companion that Morisot and Cassatt were expected to have when they strolled the city.

Monet and Renoir visited the town of Argenteuil over and over again in the late 1860s. They depicted Parisians picnicking, bathing, and relaxing. But Argenteuil was not just a pleasure-seeker's paradise. It was an industrial town. Monet gives us the occasional smokestack in the distance and views of railroad bridges, but the paintings are relentlessly cheerful, even if to a viewer of the time they would have looked less so, charged with the contradictions he knew existed because of his daily experience.

Renoir's gloss on Montmartre is similarly brightened. The bars, restaurants, and dance halls surely were places to have fun. But could the working-class people he painted possibly have been as permanently happy as his paintings suggest?

These laundresses, dressmakers, and florists, bricklayers, blacksmiths, and vegetable vendors worked long hours for little pay, lived in tiny, badly ventilated rooms, and died young. Renoir's rollicking *Dance at the Moulin de la Galette* is not peopled primarily with those neighborhood workers. What we see are Renoir's friends and several of his models. One historian suggests that the girls of the neighborhood had to be coaxed to pose, accepting presents and assurances that they wouldn't be cheapened by the experience. The result, as this historian adds, is a group of artists and writers slumming. Depicting the actual community would have resulted in a less radiant group. It wouldn't have been an Impressionist painting.

Paris and its suburbs shuddered with noise and dislocation. Excitement and anxiety lay side by side. Yet Impressionist paintings are filled with relentlessly young and happy people who did not work and who lived in eternal sunlight. Munch's horrifying *Scream* was twenty years down the road, and it would roar out of Norway. The retinal view in sunshine is what the Impressionists were after. It's as if their eyes needed to be ever sensate, as if they only felt secure and alive when they were looking hard at the world up close. And this view they made sublime.

French Impressionism is a bourgeois fantasy of the good life only mildly belied by the nervous brushstrokes. It is an enchanted delusion. And I'm a Jew who coveted blond boyfriends and longed for a Prince Charming à la Renoir. I also wished my mother was like his Mme Charpentier and that I could dwell in that cheery world of thick carpets, Japanese screens, and beribboned children. And I am a working-class girl who became an art historian.

I am also someone who has an acute sense of when people are lying to her, or even just bluffing. When I was a child, my mother would say "I have to go to Clare's house for something," and I'd want to scream "You don't *have* to go, you just *want* to go. Can't you say that? That you want to get away." Ken will say to me, "Don't go buy the milk, it's too heavy for you to carry." And I'll yell "Why can't you just say that you don't want me to leave right now because you'd rather I unpack my suitcase first? Why can't you just be honest and say what you mean?" He looks at me like I've gone mad.

So, disingenuousness, large or small, drives me wild, yet I'm the one who fell in love with France and Impressionism. I grew up in the dirty city of New York and would long for sunny Paris all my life. I swallowed the myth whole. The story of Paris was the fairy tale I kept believing, the lie I didn't want to interrogate. In the same way, I suppose, that I didn't want to look too closely at my father. Schapiro was the first to force the issue of Impressionism. Then the disjunction between the social history of nineteenth-century France and the way Impressionist paintings looked took its toll. And finally I moved to Paris, and that is when the picture postcard really began to fall apart.

My own obsessive urge to expose the "truth" did lead me to an artist in whom I found the same inclination, and, as is my wont, I fell in love with him completely. Edgar Degas was an irreverent and iconoclastic painter of women. Aside from his racetrack paintings, he represented *only* women when he wasn't making portraits. He drew laundresses, milliners, ballet dancers, and prostitutes. Normally people ooh and aah over his lovely dancers, charming milliners, concentrating ironers, all bathed in the bright light of day or the sizzle of artificial light. But I believe this happens because of entrenched attitudes toward Impressionism and not because of what's actually in his paintings. Yes, the light is mesmerizing, and we are enraptured. But if the writing and thinking about Impressionism included seeing what the Impressionists worked so hard to keep *out* of their work—the thicker social reality of their time—we would see something else in Degas's paintings.

If you page through popular magazines of the late nineteenth century, like the *Journal Amusant* or *Paris illustré* or *Charivari,* you will find many pictures of coquettish laundresses in some relationship to intimate apparel and male customers. The girls in the magazines are usually half undressed, their irons abandoned facedown on sheets, men slipping out the door, rumpled beds nearby. In the popular imagination, the laundress, any working-class girl, really, was fair game. It is also true that laundresses turned up weekly in people's homes to pick up their laundry. This wasn't true only of middle-class or wealthy people. *Everyone* had their laundry done.

Labor history takes another view of the laundress. Ironers, for example, worked long hours—up to fifteen and even eighteen hours a day. They ironed in overheated rooms where disease incubated. Inflammation of the abdomen and throat, bronchitis, and tuberculosis were professional illnesses. The stench was dreadful, the pay meager. Considering these work realities, it's odd that middle-class culture, most particularly in its appetite for magazine illustrations but also in many oil paintings, pictures these women as merely charming and alluring. And it is all the more surprising that Degas's paintings do not.

Degas may have used a popular, sexualized figure for his subject and may have stimulated sexual responses in his viewers, but he himself did not sexualize the women. To the contrary, his ironers are working. Their arms are stretched to show the strain, their skin is ruddy from the heat, their eyes dilated from fatigue. The space of Degas's paintings, like the space these women worked in, is cramped. He is not depicting an expansive, cheerful life. He is painting work.

Indeed, work was his subject as it was the very center of his life. Whether it was ironers, milliners, dancers, or prostitutes, Degas uses compositional devices to evoke the discomfort and intensity of concentrated labor. He contrives situations where compositional angles crush figures, cut them in half, make them slide down picture planes. He captures the heartlessness and agitation of modernity in his paintings, even if he hated much of modern life. Degas disliked democracy, for example, as a form of government; telephones put him off; he didn't enjoy traveling. On the other hand, photography fascinated him and he loved to wander the city that had become modern Paris.

Degas's *A Woman Seated Beside a Vase of Flowers* didn't let me down. Or, shall we say, it didn't lie to me. Degas was a great painter of women, and he could be a good friend to women as well. In the fall and winter of 1879–1880, he and Mary Cassatt worked together on prints. She used his tools and etching press. They also went to the Louvre together. Degas did a lovely etching of her there with her sister, Lydia, seated nearby.

Edgar Degas, *Ironers*, ca. 1884, Musée d'Orsay, Paris

Cassatt's back is to the viewer, but it's obvious from her silhouette that she's stylish and attractive at thirty-five years old to Degas's forty-five. Judging from Degas's paintings of her trying on hats, they also visited her milliner.

Degas's one official-looking portrait of Cassatt disarms with its honesty. He brushed the background in fiercely and abstractly, but her face and body are delineated in detail. She leans forward, her hands relaxed in her lap; her face, far from pretty, is pensive, the chin cozy in the dark mauve-colored bow that matches her hat. The face rivets our attention, like the face in *A Woman Seated Beside a Vase of Flowers*. Cassatt is intelligent and melancholy, solitary and resilient. She was known to be an acerbic woman who did not leave her paintings or her art collection to her family because they were so vocally antifeminist.

Degas was also friends with Suzanne Valadon. She and her mother arrived in Paris from the countryside near Limoges around 1870, when the girl was five. They were peasants. By the time Valadon met Degas, she was an artist's model and had herself begun to draw. He was already a mature elder artist and a confirmed bachelor. He sent her several letters in the late 1890s. "It is now nearly a month and I have not answered your good wishes for the New Year," he writes. "I have a small commission for you from one of my friends." And again, "Thank you for your good wishes, terrible Maria, all the more because I have need of them. . . . It is necessary, in spite of the illness of your son, for you to start bringing me again some wicked and supple drawings." And, "I am writing to remind you again, that once you are up and about you must . . . think of nothing but work, of utilizing the rare talent, that I am proud to see in you. . . . "

For years, it is this Degas who interests me and whom I write about: the friend of Cassatt and mentor to Valadon; the painter of working-class women, of the anxiety and toil the other Impressionists were so determined to leave out of the picture. But it was bound to happen that one day I would be forced to acknowledge what I was leaving out of my own picture, so that I could continue admiring Degas: that this man who painted women better than any other artist I know was a cheap and ordinary anti-Semite.

Pissarro was the only Jewish artist in the Impressionist group, and he was also the one with whom Degas worked most closely, though he wasn't Degas's only Jewish friend. They experimented with printing techniques and planned, along with Cassatt, to produce the magazine *Le Jour et La Nuit*. Yet after Pissarro's death, Degas wrote this to his friend Henri Rouart: "So, he has died, the poor old wandering Jew. . . . What has he been thinking since the nasty [Dreyfus] affair, what did he think of the embarrassment one felt . . . in his company? Did he ever say a word to you? . . . Did he think only of going back to the times when we were pretty nearly unaware of his terrible race?"

Pissarro and Degas spent so much time working together. Did the physical contact bother Degas? If they took a coffee together in a café, did Degas observe habits that repulsed him? Did he think Pissarro used his hands too much in conversation?

The Dreyfus Affair stretched from 1894 to 1906, and to this day it remains the point of departure in discussions about French anti-Semitism. For French Jews, as one writer puts it, the affair remains a "symbol of their always-precarious status as citizens." Before France's collaboration with the Nazis in 1940, there was nothing that stained France's image more. Ken said to me recently that the threat a Jew feels in France is emblematic of "a crack in the foundation of the Republic." And, he continued, "Jews must be really hard for the French, because we've historically been stateless, and the French so love their State." The French don't understand Jews. They can't.

Alfred Dreyfus came from a wealthy Alsatian family whose fortune had been made in textile manufacturing. In 1894, he began working in the War Office in Paris. In middle or late September of that year, a piece of paper, which would become so notorious that it would simply be known as *"le bordereau"* (the memorandum), turned up in a wastepaper basket of the counterespionage branch of the Army. This memorandum was a list of French military documents that had allegedly been handed over to the Germans. The search for the traitor began in secret. To many an observer, "what settled the fate of Dreyfus was the fact that he was a Jew and as such a rare—possibly unique—phenomenon on the General Staff." There was no evidence against Dreyfus. The handwriting of the memorandum was not his.

Colonel Hubert-Joseph Henry, a known anti-Semite, leaked the details of these events to Edmond Drumont, who, in his anti-Semitic newspaper *La Libre Parole* on November 1, 1894, named Dreyfus the traitor. Drumont wrote: "The affair will be hushed up because this officer is a Jew. . . . He was arrested two weeks ago. He has made a full confession. There is *absolute proof* that he sold our military secrets to Germany."

But there was *no* proof and there was no confession. The suggestion that Jews had the kind of power in the Army necessary to hush up such an event was absurd, an anti-Semitic phantasm. But the whirlwind was sown. Incredibly, Dreyfus was condemned. He was publicly degraded before a crowd of twenty thousand in the courtyard of the Ecole Militaire on January 5, 1895. His insignia were stripped from his cap and uniform, his sword broken. He was sentenced to life imprisonment in the infamous prison on Devil's Island in French

Guiana. The Affair almost resulted in civil war, so high did passions ride on both sides.

Anti-Dreyfusards were, in general, antimodernist in inclination. They fantasized about an earlier time when France was *La France éternelle,* and the inconveniences of democratic government were banished in favor of an enlightened monarchy. The affair ranged Republicans against anti-Republicans, people for and against the Church and the military. The journalist Drumont played a major role even before his fraudulent article condemning Dreyfus. An early series in his newspaper was titled "Jews in the Army." And in 1886, he had published *La France Juive,* which, according to one writer, "had given the anti-Semites a text-book."

La Libre Parole was Edgar Degas's favorite newspaper. His maid, Zoë, read it to him at mealtimes. He relished the details. "Did Degas think of [his childhood friend] Ludovic Halévy," one historian asks, "when he heard such sentiments as, 'for God, the nation and the extermination of the Jews,' . . . or 'French honor against Jewish gold'?" Or of the good-natured Pissarro, perhaps? In an article of 1898, a poet and journalist wrote, "When a model in [Degas's] studio expressed doubt of Dreyfus's guilt, Degas screamed at her, 'You are Jewish . . . you are Jewish. . . .' 'But I am a Protestant. . . .' 'Never mind . . . get dressed and get out!'" Pissarro sent a copy of this article to his son Lucien, referring to Degas, his old friend and colleague, as "the ferocious anti-Semite."

Intellectuals, artists, and politicians who signed a petition demanding vindication of Dreyfus included Proust, Charles Péguy, Léon Blum, Georges Clemenceau, Jean Jaurès, Anatole France, André Gide, Cassatt, Monet, Pissarro, and Paul

Signac. Against Dreyfus were Léon Daudet, Jules Verne, Maurice Barrès, Charles Maurras, Renoir, Rodin, Cézanne, and Degas. "Jews shouldn't be allowed to become so important in France," said Renoir. He didn't want to exhibit with "the Jew Pissarro."

The affair did not end with Dreyfus's degradation and imprisonment. Due to the uneasy conscience of an army officer, Lieutenant-Colonel Picquart; to Dreyfus's wife and brother; and to the writer Emile Zola's open letter "J'accuse," published in Georges Clemenceau's newspaper, *L'Aurore*, the case stayed open. Zola's letter appeared on January 13, 1898, when Major Marie-Charles Esterhazy, the man who turned out to be the real spy and against whom charges were brought, was absurdly acquitted. Zola accused the army and the government of a cover-up. He wrote: "My duty is to speak out. I do not want to be an accomplice in this travesty. My nights will otherwise be haunted by the specter of this innocent man far away, suffering the most horrible of tortures for a crime he did not commit. . . . I accuse . . . the first council of war of having violated the law . . . and I accuse the second council of war of having covered this illegality . . . knowingly acquitting a guilty man."

Anti-Semitic riots broke out in the hundreds all over France and in Algeria. "A lowly priest in Poitou," we are told, "said that he 'would happily chant the Requiem for the last of the yids'"; while other contributors poured venom on "Jewish vermin," "Jewish microbes," and "the Jewish cancer."

Zola was tried for libel and found guilty. He fled to England, where he died of gas asphyxiation five years later. He was probably murdered. It was only after I learned all this that I realized why Zola was considered such a hero in my house when I was growing up.

One would think such events would make French Jews leave France. It didn't. France was the first country to give them citizenship, and they were perhaps more grateful than they should have been. Even after World War II, the Jews went through amazing contortions to forgive the French and blame the Germans.

———

So, Monsieur Degas, my hero, there it is. You were a miserable anti-Semite. Now I can say it. But *why* were you? When your hatred flared, what provoked it? A dealer who didn't pay you enough? Did you wonder why "they" were so good at business, when your own family failed so miserably? Were you envious of Pissarro's and your old friend Halévy's loving families? Did you long to possess their personal confidence? Scholars' answers vary. But what's the difference? You were who you were. If you had been around in the 1940s, you would have turned your back on the Jews being rounded up by the French police and sent to Auschwitz. And in the 1950s, you would have done the same for the Algerians. And today you would probably vote for Le Pen.

Many people in France—most, perhaps—are anti-Semitic. "Oh, it was only a joke," my plumber says to me after telling me an anti-Semitic story. This anti-Semitism, like Degas's, poisons French society. Its very casualness normalizes it. In Degas's painting *At the Stock Exchange*, painted before the Affair, his ordinary anti-Semitism is obvious. We see men in top hats and beards, long pointy noses, gargoylish faces, clumsy hands pawing each other. These are clichés about Jews: vulgar, ugly, money-obsessed, subhuman. Not French.

And yet Degas, a miserable anti-Semite, told the truth about women and work, and made paintings that never cease to give me pleasure. If I were to label them politically, I would call them progressive. Degas was not only an evil force in history. It is impossible to say that. And Renoir, another vile anti-Semite, lied about the social realities of his day in his paintings but painted a world I often long to step into, a world where happiness never goes away. I still love all those paintings as I continue to love France. But I must admit that it is no longer the generous, sun-drenched country I thought it was, and the dissimulating has begun to bother me.

CHAPTER 4

What Glory

T he Roaring Twenties—or, in French, *les années folles,* the Wild, Mad Years: Americans wrote their hearts out in one part of Montparnasse while Eastern European Jewish artists painted and sculpted a few streets away. Jazz, brought over by African Americans, set hearts and feet thumping. Blacks, Jews, artists, writers. The French threw open their arms to foreigners and were going just a little bit wild. Even women. I had been waiting for the return of Olympe de Gouges, feminist leader of the Revolution and writer in 1791 of *The Rights of Woman and the Female Citizen.* Now she was back, but in modern dress.

By the 1920s, Colette was finally writing her sensuous adventures under her own name and not her husband Willy's.

African American performer Josephine Baker wowed Paris
with her roguish dance routines. Talented, outspoken women
were everywhere. There was Tamara Lempicka, painter of
hardness and modernity; Nancy Cunard, ocean-liner heiress
and publisher. And of course Gertrude Stein, experimental
writer, salonnière, and famously sexist lesbian and anti-
Semitic Jew.

Hemlines went up. Corsets were tossed. Paul Poiret's
loose-fitting clothing, introduced in the early years of the
century, turned more glamorous and more available in the
hands of Coco Chanel. Women across class moved freely in
their unconstructed clothing and hats with no veils, no
plumes, no doodads. Elegant sleekness was what Chanel was
after. Not nearly as enchanting personally as her clothing,
she famously cringed before overweight Colette, who, she
said, "swaggers in gluttony. The whole of Saint-Tropez is
astonished."

The modern woman drove cars, planes, speedboats. She
competed in professional tennis matches. She painted,
wrote, designed buildings, made photographs. "Amateur"
was no longer a word used to describe her. There is a photo
from the 1920s of a woman at the wheel of a taxicab,
another in a Chanel dress on a motor scooter. Momentum
had been building since the late nineteenth century, when
women entered the urban workforce in large numbers as
well as being ever more present in small businesses, with
their husbands or on their own. The confidence and energy
that came with living differently from their mothers and
grandmothers, the accumulation of these acts produced the
woman of the Twenties. In addition, women were forced

during World War I to do men's jobs. They didn't simply forget that experience in the next decade.

Girls cut their hair *à la garçonne*—in a boyish fashion—after a best-selling book of the same title by Victor Margueritte, published in 1922. Women in *La Garçonne* dressed like boys, and the central character took both girls and boys as lovers. The author was expelled from the Legion of Honor, but the books sold over a million copies, and he wrote two sequels.

The eighteenth-century salonnières never had this kind of effect. Nor did they want to. Amidst the aromas and textures of pleasure and privilege, male desire is what they facilitated. Female desire in its larger social and cultural form had to wait for the twentieth century. And to us in the twenty-first—when sexism in fundamentalist religions threatens to make us disappear under hoods and veils and wigs and hobble us by injunctions to mother first of all—the bursting-out of that desire, in the 1920s, is all the more appealing.

The 1920s were fun for women. For one thing, it was the first time in the modern Western world that lesbians lived openly. Natalie Barney was the most public, flamboyant, and wealthy of the gay women in Paris. Her Friday-night literary salon, launched in 1909, flourished in the Twenties. Paul Claudel was a guest, and sometimes Colette. So were André Gide, Proust, Rodin, Paul Valéry, Renée Vivien, and Tamara de Lempicka. Sometimes Barney's longtime lover, the stern and scary painter Romaine Brooks, came by.

Then there was the intriguingly original photographer Claude Cahun and her girlfriend and fellow artist Marcel Moore; Sylvia Beach, the famously generous publisher and owner of Shakespeare and Company, and her companion,

Adrienne Monnier, owner of the bookstore *La Maison des amis des livres*, a center of the French avant-garde; *New Yorker* correspondent Janet Flanner; and the great photographer of New York, Berenice Abbott. And these are just the famous women. How wonderful it must have been. All those girls and books and art and conversation and love. And Paris.

Daily lives would be daily lives, of course, but many French people shook, rattled, and rolled in these years, and the tunes were mostly American. Jazz, *le hot*, lit up Right Bank nightlife, and the French, taking those rhythms to heart, wove their fantasies around them. Whether you lived quietly and worked as a waiter in a bar, or cleaned rooms in a hotel, or sold vegetables, or were a cop or a writer, you knew where the dance spots were, and you probably were aware of African Americans in town.

Of course, there was plenty of outrage about the effects of this American music and dancing. One teachers' organization condemned the "exotic fantasies executed to the sound of savage music." Doctors said the dances brought on "dangerous illnesses, like . . . cystitis in women and impotence in men."

You can't stop kids from dancing, though. And shouldn't. I remember seeing photos of my parents sitting at nightclub tables, eyes wide, lips parted, smiling and drinking with friends, at the ready to jump up and charge back onto the dance floor. Black-and-white photos with crisp edges and tuxedo contrasts, bodies close together. I grew up admiring my long-legged mother and dapper father, grabbing everyone's attention at weddings and bar mitzvahs with their rumbas, foxtrots, and even their rambunctious Charleston pulled up out of their own teenage years.

One day, I watched my mother in my grandparents' living room in Hurleyville. We were waiting for news about Grandpa, who had had a heart attack and was in the hospital. She was listening to the radio in the background, bouncing her foot unconsciously to the beat. She reached for my father's hand, urging him to forget his worries for a while. He pushed her away.

———

"She made her entry entirely nude except for a pink flamingo feather between her limbs," wrote Janet Flanner about Josephine Baker's debut in *La Revue Nègre* in 1925 at the Théâtre des Champs Elysées. "She was being carried upside down," Flanner continues, "and doing the split on the shoulder of a black giant. Midstage he paused, and with his long fingers holding her basket-wise around the waist, swung her in a slow cartwheel to the stage floor where she stood . . . an unforgettable female ebony statue. A scream of salutation spread through the theater."

Langston Hughes worked as a short-order cook in Montmartre in these years. "The cream of the Negro musicians then in France . . . would weave out music," he wrote, "that would almost make your heart stand still. . . . Blues in the rue Pigalle. Black and laughing, heart-breaking blues in the Paris dawn, pounding like a pulse-beat, moving like the Mississippi!"

My Uncle Dave stopped off in Paris just ten years later, on his way to Spain. He was looking forward to fighting for the Spanish Republic alongside African Americans. He was proud of it. The Abraham Lincoln Brigade was the first integrated American fighting force in history. There were about eighty

African American volunteers, and one of them, Oliver Law, briefly became their commander in the late spring of 1937. Canute Frankson, a black autoworker from Detroit, wrote to a friend, "On the battlefields of Spain we fight for the preservation of democracy. Here, we're laying the foundation for world peace, and for the liberation of my people, and of the human race. Here . . . there is no color line, no discrimination, no race hatred. There's only one hate, and that is the hate for fascism." Salaria Kee, a black nurse, wanted to work with the American Red Cross to help flood victims in her native Ohio. "They told me they had no place for me," she told an interviewer, "that the color of my skin would make me more trouble than I'd be worth to them." A friend suggested Spain to her, and that's where she went. Blacks had to leave America to feel like human beings.

But the French have always had a special, if paradoxical, affection for African Americans. More so than for their own blacks arriving from French protectorates and colonies like Madagascar, Tahiti, Martinique, and Guinea. American blacks were somehow New World to Old Europe and Old Africa. They were "young," like America herself. Then there was the history of slavery in America, which the French could abhor and feel superior to—the French, who had fought so hard for their own Republic, which they took to be more radical than ours. And their Revolution, unlike ours, *had* abolished slavery. Segregation was illegal in France. Period. Blacks came to America in chains. Not so in France, the French said. There's always a contest between French and Americans, a sizing-up and measuring.

Paris in the 1920s must have amazed American blacks. Just

sixty years after the American Civil War, they never had to think twice about entering a theater or restaurant, a hotel or a toilet. "The idea that a black man could not only openly court a white woman," writes one historian, "but then challenge a white man who protested must have seemed like a fantasy in 1920s America, one that bore the stamp 'made in France.'" It still does. The numbers of interracial couples one sees in France today astonish Americans. This, ironically, does not mean that the French are not racist, but only that they make excuses for love. All the same, this experience changes them fundamentally.

Many black GIs spent time in France during World War I and passed through Paris on their way home. Soon after the war, Senator James Vardaman of Mississippi advised that "every community in Mississippi . . . led by the bravest and best white men . . . should pick out these suspicious characters—those military, French-women–ruined negro soldiers and let them understand that they are under surveillance. . . ." Lynchings in America jumped from fifty-seven in 1918 to seventy-seven in 1919. "Ten of these were black veterans," a historian tells us. Those black soldiers experienced something in France that many could only give up with their lives. By the 1920s, a revived Ku Klux Klan had four million members in the United States. In those same years, France was deep in its love affair with American blacks. Though, to be sure, blacks remained exotic, and, if adored, they were also objectified. It was rarely, as a friend put it to me, that the French thought they were "the same as us."

France was in love with America in general. The French marveled at American skyscrapers and cowboys, chewing gum and colored toilet paper, grapefruit and disposable Gillette razor blades. They were amazed by pictures of porcelain bathroom fixtures and the numbers of automobiles on American roads. There was even a debate in the newspapers about the quality of their cocktails. One American living in Paris said, "I was urged by my friends at the Caveau bar to mix an American cocktail so that they would be in a better position to judge between the xenophobes who denounced the New World *apéritif* and those milder critics who said it made no difference what Americans drank before the kind of meals they habitually ate."

The Wild Years! And I haven't even mentioned the fabulous immigrant Jewish artists in Montparnasse. Jacques Lipshitz, Chaim Soutine, Chana Orloff, Jules Pascin, Moise Kisling, Chagall. And Man Ray from New York. It was only fifteen years since the end of the Dreyfus Affair, yet Jews kept arriving in Paris. Like my father, they grew up with the myth of cultured, egalitarian France. And gorgeous Paris. And oh, those women! The Dreyfus Affair is an aberration, they told themselves, recalling instead Liberty, Equality, Fraternity. And France was, after all, the first country in the world to give Jews citizenship. Well, the French capitulation to the German didn't stop me from coming to France either. And staying.

In neighborhoods like Montparnasse, one heard Russian, Polish, English, Japanese, Portuguese, Spanish, Italian. France never knew such cultural and ethnic variety. One writer remarked that his local grocer carried "cassia, cloves, caraway and coriander, mace, cumin, anise, capers, cardamom, chervil, basil, tarragon savor, curcuma, fennel and other treasures of

Arabia, but on days his business took him near the Madeleine, [he] . . . would stare and sigh at bean sprouts from China, canned tamales from Mexico, fabulous products in cardboard boxes from America, labeled 'Quaker Oats.'"

And the American writers in Paris! They created what was one of the most famous literary scenes of all time, although when I first learned about them, there were no women. Feminists found Stein, Flanner, Djuna Barnes, and Kay Boyle. But you can't disdain a list that includes Hemingway, Dos Passos, and Fitzgerald. Americans were writing and drinking, freezing and drinking, dancing and drinking, some deep wonderment and desire blowing through them. They hungered for life abroad, sick of American vacuity and vulgarity. They landed in the Twenties in France—some of them, like Hemingway, having participated in World War I—and for the most part they had a very good ride indeed.

However self-contained and elegant the French seem, they know how to run out of control and how to get what they want. They don't do things by half measures. And in the 1920s, the cultural floodgates broke. Here's a description of a Dada performance of 1920 in Paris : "[Tristan] Tzara was introduced to the public. He read aloud a newspaper article, while an electric bell kept ringing so that nobody could hear what he said." Tzara describes an event soon after that, where "for the first time in the history of the world, people threw at us not only eggs, vegetables and pennies, but beefsteaks as well. It was a very huge success." Irreverence, irrationality, chaos. This is the Twenties. Or rather, it was the only Twenties I had heard about.

I do begin to wonder, though, how it happened that such

a triumphant and expansive period could have culminated, a decade later, in the darkest time of French history, the collaboration with the Nazis. Not that a country's trajectory is predictable. Consider how the destruction of New York's Twin Towers on September 11, 2001 altered America. But the fact is, it didn't alter it completely. The germ of what we became in America was already in us—Christian fundamentalism, suspicion of outsiders, presidential infringement on personal liberties, indifference to international law. It occurs to me that, even in the glorious Twenties, there was something already in the French that could take them to bed with the Germans. That's when the decade began to look different to me.

—

France is the only country whose government made a pact with the Germans that allowed the Third Reich to actually govern part of their country. I find this an unbearable fact, even now at a sixty-six-year distance. I don't want it to have happened, just as I don't want Degas to have been an anti-Semite. When American friends say to me, Well, the French, they are famous anti-Semites, I get angry. I pull out my statistics: 75 percent of all Dutch Jews were killed in the Holocaust, only 25 percent of French Jews. France isn't the *biggest* hater of Jews in the world. But I'm kidding myself. I'm angry, and I'm heartbroken.

My disappointment congeals slowly over years. Probably it was always there, but I didn't have to look at it until I moved to France and personally experienced the effects of their history and their racism. Then I learned that they betrayed their own inspiring ideas about freedom and equality—ideas that I grew up with, and that I was taught France had invented. The French Republic, with its goal of economic, social, and political equality, was partnered in my mind to my father's love of Zola, my mother's pleasure in Impressionism, my uncle's death in Spain. And yes, with regicide. That too. Bloody heads stuck on poles. The French are not timid, and frankly I've always liked that about them. They know how to get angry in the cause of justice. No middle-of-the-road American moderation for them.

How did my father, who was so very alert to his marginality and vulnerability as a Jew, always ready to see an enemy in any Gentile's face—how did he happen to forget about French anti-Semitism? What was the lure that made him forget? Something about France pulled him irresistibly in and held him. Sometimes I think it was his own brother's face. Dave, with his wavy blond hair and gentle ways, the only son who was an idealist, the brother my father smashed. He never gave the boy's letters to their parents. Like William Styron's Nat Turner—who, in the slave uprising he instigated, could only kill one person, the plantation owner's daughter, whom he loved—so my father betrayed the person he loved most in the world, and the boy who represented hope to him. But I think Dave's optimism, willy-nilly, infected my father. He longed to find some of his brother in himself, to believe in something, to have that confidence that would free him. He wanted to believe that people could be good. He wanted anti-Semitism to go away and to take his hatred with it.

The fantasy of France, its politics and culture, soothed my father as his brother had before he could no longer remember him, so he brushed French anti-Semitism aside. Yet he said, when Ken and I bought our Paris apartment, "Why did you do that?" Was he wondering then where I had gotten the nerve to live amongst the goyim? Was he still afraid after all?

Stranger and more embattled foreigners than I have loved France. Ferhat Abbas, an early leader of Algerian independence, was an ardent believer in the Revolution of 1789. He was sure that France would recognize the Muslim right to Algeria in the name of liberty, equality, fraternity. Mohammed Larbi Madi, another Algerian leader, wrote in a letter from prison, "I am seeking the France I learned of in school. . . ." Me too. And at my father's side.

James Baldwin anguished over America in a similar way. "I was forced to admit something I had always hidden from myself," he wrote in 1955, "which the American Negro has had to hide from himself as the price of his public progress; that I hated and feared white people." Yet, two pages on, he erupted with, "I love America more than any other country in the world, and, exactly for this reason, I insist on the right to criticize her perpetually." I think I love France with a passion as deep and conflicted as Baldwin's passion for America.

When Zola wrote books about laundresses and construction workers, prostitutes and coal miners, he was writing about people whose personal dignity became a fact only with the birth of the French Republic, when the power of politics and suffrage took the place of wealth and privilege. Everybody's life would be worth something. There would be traces of each individual at city halls in every town in France. Birth certificates, death certificates, marriage certificates. Each person's passage would be marked by the State. Every life would be valuable and would resonate with their great country's history, *la Gloire*, that is France for its citizens. And for me and so many others too. Republicanism is France's triumph, the glory of its Revolution. The French and those who love France cherish this history.

My uncle disembarked in Le Havre on his way to Spain. He and Bill Wheeler, whom he'd met on the ship over, spent a day and night in Paris on the Right Bank. They took a walk around the city in the evening. It was a mild spring night, delicate and sweet. Late May 1938. They walked near Père Lachaise Cemetery. Bill had been here before. "There's a wall in there where they executed men from the Commune," he said to my uncle. "You know that Civil War they had here in Paris at the end of the last century. I've seen pictures. And then afterwards the men and women lined up in coffins. Terrible. It's a violent country."

"More than America?"

"Much more."

They continued along the edge of the cemetery, south to the *Nation* area. "There's a famous street near here," said Bill, where a lot of radical workers lived and worked, "Saint Antoine or something."

They walked around *Nation*, and started down the street, Faubourg St. Antoine. They stopped and had a beer. Bill nodded at some workers at the other end of the bar and they, smiling, raised their glasses: *"Viva la Republica!"* Across the distance of different languages surged the mutual hope for the fledgling Spanish democracy. The French men knew who Dave and Bill were. What would young Americans have been doing in that part of Paris, that Communist neighborhood where tourists never came? These fresh-faced and open, naïve perhaps, and oddly good-natured Americans. It was obvious that they were on their way to Spain. Dave and Bill lifted their glasses: *"Viva la Republica!"* And added, *"No pasaran!"*

Bill told me they were brought through France to the Pyrenees by French Communists.

My concierge will not be condescended to. Nor my plumber. And can anyone who has wandered a French market imagine talking down to the man who sells eight varieties of mushrooms, ten kinds of potatoes, and all sorts of fresh greens, carrots, turnips, parsley, and dill? And then there are the waiters. Not your American type, biding his time until he can find a role on Broadway, take up a seat in an orchestra, waiting until she can get her novel published. Waiters in France are there for life, because it is a trade that is respected and enjoyed. They go to school to learn it, as do chambermaids. Everybody is important, and everybody's work and contribution to their country is important. That's the French Republican promise.

Zola staked his professional life on the defense not only of the *Jew* Dreyfus—who himself was sick and tired of the brouhaha about the fact that he was Jewish and would have liked to swat it away like an annoying fly—but more important of the Republican values pro-Dreyfusards believed in: a written constitution, a nationally elected President, a country governed by laws, not patronage, reason, not superstition.

For my younger self, Impressionism was part of that great France. Here were handsome, hardy people gathered around food- and wine-laden picnic tables, lingering in perfect sunny landscapes, meandering along country lanes where they might encounter a neighbor, stare up at a lazy plume of smoke, inhale the scents of loam and leaves and hay. This was pleasure for everyone. It didn't say "Jews, keep out!" It wasn't the little town of Hurleyville, whose two white churches scared me so much that when I went to practice the piano in the unmarked synagogue at the edge of town, I was afraid to go without my Grandpa.

Be French and you will be equal, the French say. And anyone who shares our values and who is being harassed in their own country is welcome here. That is the promise. To this day, they accept more immigrants than the United States does. But they also say: Be Other at home, that's your business. In public, you must be French, and you will be one of us. No declaration of Otherness, no telltale signs, certainly no public pride in your heritage. The Jews obeyed, and look what happened to them. The Germans said to the French: Get rid of them, and they did it, and so well that there were fewer German soldiers and SS in France than in any other occupied country.

This is what it felt like to an eight-year-old Jewish girl in Paris on July 16, 1942: "My father knew he was going to be picked up. . . . He was rabbi of a small synagogue. . . . He had left home very early that day to warn as many Jews as he could to go into hiding immediately. Then he came home and waited. . . . He waited and prayed to God that they would come for him, as long as his wife and children could be saved. . . . Four in the afternoon. Someone knocks. . . . We never did see my father again. Or get any news of him, either, except a card sent from Drancy [a stadium where Jews were held], written in purple ink, with a stamp on it bearing Marshal Pétain's picture." It wasn't their father's handwriting.

Here is a question that haunts me and that I know is at the heart of this book: Was France's lightning capitulation to Germany in 1939 aberrant or typical? When I ask if a painting loves me, I know what I am really asking is, Does France love me? Or will she betray me again, as she did in 1940?

And now I ask: What is the relationship between the feverishly open Twenties and what happened at the end of the 1930s? It turns out that the answer lies not in these years themselves but in an earlier time, in World War I. In the war that produced the Wild Years, but also produced another 1920s, entirely distinct from the one I have been writing about.

———

The French were ruined by the war, even though their side won it. They never recovered because they never acknowledged what it made them do later. They couldn't admit, probably didn't know, how those war years seeped into them and invaded their being. The horrors of the war churned in them and turned their wounds into hatred. The wildness of the 1920s scarcely touched most French people. Bitterness, fear, and longing, rather, filled their emotional landscape.

World War I was not a war I knew much about. Yes, Jake Barnes's impotence in Hemingway's *A Sun Also Rises* was related to it, and the Dada movement too. And I knew something about the trenches. Let's say that I knew this history mechanically, by rote, a lesson I learned at school. It didn't matter to me, though. But I was irritated by all the World War I monuments in France I stumbled across. At first I just noticed them the way one half-sees statues in Central Park of General Sherman or Alice in Wonderland. They were so much bric-a-brac. But there is almost no French town or village where one doesn't find such a monument. In a country smaller than Texas, there are thirty-eight thousand of them. The state encouraged and subsidized their construction. They were built swiftly, many being finished by 1922. Sometimes they were put up even before the war was over. *During* the war. "Before the armistice," one historian writes, "the dead had already become the object of such a cult, with demonstrations in their honor by maimed and incapacitated comrades. . . . Could a cult born when it was still possible that the war might end in defeat have been a cult of victory?" Quite a question.

These monuments were the first sign to me that modern history was a different story in France than in America. World War II is the war of the twentieth century for us: the landings on the beaches at Normandy; the raising of the flag at Iwo Jima; Generals Patton and Eisenhower; *Life* magazine photographs of Buchenwald. Americans saved the Jews. What was left of them. That was the story afterward, anyway.

In my family, after Dave's death in Spain, the Communists were banished as a subject. So we didn't talk about Russia's part in the Allied victory or the liberation of the camps. One of Grandma's sisters-in-law kept going to Russia in the late Forties and Fifties, and she put her two cents in and nobody silenced her, but Russia was a subject we generally avoided.

My father in his cynicism went even further. One day at dinner with his parents, he muttered, "Nothing is worth dying for. Look at those guys who came back from Spain. They're millionaires today, and my brother is dead. . . ." His mother fixed him with a look that silenced him. He kept a shoe box with the letters and photographs, the harmonica, on a high shelf in his closet. Was he saying his brother died for nothing? So now my father did have to care about anything or anyone either? Was this how he rationalized his self-absorption? Across his dead brother's body?

What I remember after the war is that we celebrated what America did, led by the great Franklin Delano Roosevelt, and that we had confronted the evils of the Old World. Only later had it become public what Roosevelt *wouldn't* do for the Jews, like allowing the ship *St. Louis*, with 937 Jews escaping Germany, to enter an American port in 1939, or bombing the rail lines leading to Auschwitz when he and most other leaders knew that its mission was to destroy European Jewry.

In my mind, World War I has never been a war that ranged good against evil—a war that *mattered*—the way the other war did. So every time I come upon a World War I monument, it annoys me. They are so plain and soulless amidst the extreme beauty of French villages and countryside. But then I begin to wonder when I see them, Where are the World War II memorials? What about the Holocaust? Where are the Jews in French war stories? Or the Communists, the socialists, Resistance fighters? Where is World War II? If you look hard, you will find names of the World War II dead at the bottom or back of a village's World War I monument. A few names. Many fewer French people died in that war.

I begin to realize that something is buried in that second war that the French can't tolerate, and that the first war takes up more space for good reasons but for shameful ones, too. It is constantly pulled out and remembered, and transformed into something digestible. It becomes part of the unexamined and repeated recitation of French history, along with Charlemagne, Joan of Arc, and Charles de Gaulle. It becomes a fetish.

The war does begin to get to me though. At first it's because of Pat Barker's great trilogy about it from an English vantage point, *Regeneration*, *The Eye in the Door*, *The Ghost Road*. There is Siegfried Sassoon, the poet and aristocratic Jew who, after great bravery in the field, becomes a pacifist. The psychiatrist Dr. William Rivers—like Sassoon, a real figure, fictionalized by Barker—brooding but patriotic, treating shell-shocked men and pushing them, including Sassoon, back to the front. And there is Barker's invention, the working-class, angry, terribly sensual, and street-smart Billy Prior. All three of them alive, and dying. I begin to understand.

One fifth of the French population fought in the war. Almost every family lost someone. No one had ever seen or imagined such horrors. In the fall of 1914, France "lost in dead, missing, wounded, or prisoners some 850,000 men." By the Armistice, that figure was more than double. One historian writes about the battle of Verdun, "The Germans had massed more than 1,200 artillery pieces, or one gun for every twenty-five yards of the front. On July 15 [1916], they fired twenty-one million howitzer shells . . . and no doubt even more shells of smaller caliber, or roughly one shell for every square yard of the battlefield. . . . Like Auschwitz, in World War II, Verdun came to symbolize a breach of the limits of the human condition. . . ."

I read about men trudging back into villages after days of pounding at the front. One soldier remembers that "They were like convicts just released from the prison of war, and when they looked up at the roofs of the village one read in their eyes unspeakable depths of pain. As they raised their faces, their features seemed trapped in the dirt and twisted by suffering. Their mute faces seemed to cry out in horror at the incredible awfulness of their martyrdom."

Archibald MacLeish, the young American poet in Paris in the early 1920s, wrote, "The thing I used to notice in Paris was the total absence of the young." France's lost generation. A million and a quarter French soldiers dead, half a million civilians. A million more permanently crippled. And the war was fought largely on French soil, on that sacred, beloved, miraculously fertile French soil. Scars remain to this day—sunken paths cut through fields, the ghosts of trenches, an occasional unexploded mine. And they won the war.

"Let it be over soon! No matter how it ends," blurted out the child Simone de Beauvoir to her mother.

In Hemingway's *A Farewell to Arms*, the young American Frederic Henry talks to an equally young priest during a lull in battle:

"What will happen?" [asks Henry]. . . .

"I do not know but I do not think it can go on much longer."

"What will happen?"

"They will stop fighting."

The priest thinks that both sides, seeing the madness, will stop. Henry disagrees. The Austrians won't stop because winners don't call it quits, he says. The priest continues.

"You discourage me."

"I can only say what I think."

"Then you think it will go on and on? Nothing will ever happen?"

"I don't know. . . ."

"I had hoped for something."

"Defeat?"

"No. Something more."

"There isn't anything more. Except victory. It may be worse."

What is Hemingway's premonition?

You can watch film footage of the battle of Gallipoli. The Allies lost about 187,000 men, the Turks 211,000. For nothing. Both sides today agree that it was for nothing. The story was the same at the Somme—600,000 French and British dead, the same number of Germans. Declared a "victory" for the Allies because they advanced eight kilometers—150,000 lives for each kilometer. The whole war was for nothing. Just a lot of political maneuvering for national and financial gain. Is that glory?

Even today there are French people who remember dolorous maiden aunts, the women who would have married all those lost men, hovering at the edges of family gatherings, tending other people's children, keeping other people's homes. All the women in black, gliding, murmuring through the country, their silhouettes shaping the desires of generations, of what is possible and what is not. My friend Chantal tells me that "'la transmission' went missing after the war," what only one generation can give to another. This was a generation that went missing.

And among those who returned, so many damaged beyond

repair. Hemingway, living in Paris just afterward, noticed veterans in his local café: "I . . . saw the quality of their artificial eyes and the degree of skill with which their faces had been reconstructed. There was always an almost iridescent shiny cast about the considerably reconstructed face, rather like that of a well packed ski run. . . ." Hemingway is describing the *gueules cassées*, the shattered faces of soldiers, a subject made excruciatingly present in François Dupeyron's 2001 film, *La Chambre des Officiers.*

Elliot Paul, another American in Paris, described a devout young widow who now must rely on the promises of the afterlife: "[She] is quietly starving and sitting very still in a chair, alone in a room with lace on the cushions, lace antimacassars on the chairs. . . . This young woman, dutiful and obedient from birth, is trying to dull [her] . . . bereavement with a bewildered hope that she has not been misled about the future life . . . and that her resurrected young husband will not be a *gueule cassée* throughout Eternity."

How these ruined faces must have haunted the French, who so worship beauty. Their churches' gargoyles may be hideous, and Victor Hugo's hunchback and Cocteau's beast as well, but beauty is the divine French destination. Small surprise that it was French plastic surgeons who were the first, in November 2005, to successfully perform a face transplant.

The war threw the French into bereavement and paralysis. And regression. They experienced its wounds as a body will, for a long time. American blacks live with slavery, Jews with the Holocaust. World War I is France's holocaust. After the war—the winning of the war, mind you—the French would hold their country in their arms, like the body of Christ taken down from the cross. They could not stop weeping. So many had died or been ruined as they fought over a few meters, living and dying in dank, vermin-ridden trenches. And nearly a half million bodies were never found. "Missing" or "presumed dead" was all the families got. This was modern warfare, bodies blown to pieces, blown away. Perhaps this is why in so many films about war there are scenes of the dead being pulled to "safety." At least to have the bodies. I never thought about what it meant to my grandparents and to my father that Dave disappeared in Spain.

The French called their bombed northeastern towns, rich with their architectural and cultural heritage, *villes martyrs*, martyred cities. Towns like Reims, Arras, Soissons. Their scarred lands and destroyed historic buildings anthropomorphized into flesh and blood. In 1920, Joan of Arc was canonized and then commemorated in a national holiday. She, who would drive the English out of France, was the modern-day symbol of the French resisting the Germans—and of what it had cost them to do so.

This war created the wildness of the Twenties, the hunger to break out, to be new and fresh, imaginative, and open. And then perhaps maybe, maybe war would go away and never come back again. Many people wanted to simply forget the war and the culture that created its heartless stupidities and desecration. But the jazz, the dancing, the international art scene, the short hair and short skirts, didn't touch most people in France. Any more than, in 1960s America, the drugs and flower children and great sex and political rage figured in the experience of most Americans, who were simply living their ordinary lives, going to church and voting for Richard Nixon.

That's why they got so mad at Bill Clinton years later: He reminded them of what they hadn't been a part of, and their envy was breathtaking.

In war-ravaged France, the mourning of the vast majority went on and on, and then its outward forms stopped. But the monuments were there. A blanket of nostalgia was pulled over the land and the mood shifted. The French were determined to bring their glorious country back from despair, theirs, the oldest and grandest nation on the European continent. The family would be put firmly back in place. Women would leave their jobs and be women again, men would be men. People started rummaging in their attics. They would remake themselves in the image of their grandparents. They would take care of the country the way the peasants nourished the land, and the way the peasants, they said, won the war for them. They wanted to be told what to do, and do it simply. They were exhausted and wanted rules, no clutter, no confusion. Thus would they cure themselves.

They repressed the trauma, the amputated limbs, the mutilations, the devastated land, and dwindled population. Forgetting is the easiest thing in the world to do, isn't it? I would rather concentrate on contented American blacks in Paris, women taxicab drivers, and flourishing Jewish artists than think about what was going to happen in 1940. That's what the French wanted, in their own way—to cleave to a happier version of themselves.

They wanted to go home again, to the good old days, when people went about their business delivering laundry, clerking at the police station, working in brothels, running hotels, writing, policing, cooking, and cleaning. And going to church.

The church and the military would be respected. The Dreyfus Affair was revisited. People expressed their rage now at the outcome, and the fact that the military had been humiliated by a Jew. After the affair, there had been a weeding out of non-Republicans (often practicing Catholics) from the Army. French Catholics didn't forget that.

They were also simmering in anger over the separation of church and state set in motion by the Revolution and culminated in the famous law of 1905. That is when the state took control of all public education and prohibited priests from being teachers in public schools. Priests were no longer allowed to qualify for the exams required to become teachers. Laws also demanded that every congregation ask for legal authorization from the state to exist. It made all upkeep of churches the Church's responsibility. It put the burial of people in the hands of the state. Crosses were removed from law courts. Now, in the Twenties, these secularizing laws were thought to have gone too far. People wanted a return to order, to restraint, to correctness, and to respect for the past. "In 1919 for the first time under the Third Republic," one historian writes, "France had a Chamber [of government] in which there was a majority of practicing Catholics."

I know a thing or two about churches, the magnificent French cathedrals, the gigantic rotund columns that you can't reach your arms around, spaces you feel entirely safe in, sculptures of the Saved and the Damned. But who was safe and who was saved and who was damned? I know the tale told endlessly by priests worldwide about the Wandering Jew, reproduced for centuries in French pictures and stories. The Jew who was said to have mocked Jesus as he trudged through Jerusalem with his cross. For this Jews would suffer and be detested through eternity. They would never stop wandering. The very heart of anti-Semitism is the Catholic Church. I am not interested in hearing about their ruined churches.

In the 1920s, intolerant Catholicism reached into every aspect of French life. It shaped the way women would henceforward think about themselves. Babies, babies, babies are what was called for. Women must be feminine and natural. They must be what God meant them to be, mothers and wives. Forget about *"le hot"* and jobs outside the home. The need for growth in the French population was obvious, but even so, the rage at women who were seen as modern is surprising. Only socialists and feminists dared criticize natalism, the Church-supported pro-birth movement.

Women were criticized for cutting their hair short. "Throughout the decade," a historian tells us, "newspapers recorded lurid tales, including one husband in the provinces who sequestered his wife for bobbing her hair and a father who reportedly killed his daughter for the same reason. A father in Dijon sought legal action against a hairdresser in 1925 for cutting the hair of his daughter without his authority." The Twenties were not a great time for women in France. Perhaps for some who had money and education, like that famous handful on the Left Bank, but not for most. The skinny flapper was shoved off-stage.

Even Picasso was part of that Mother renewal. He drew and painted many tender mother-and-child pictures in the Twenties. Newly married in 1918, with his first child born in 1921, it's possible that he was inspired by his own domestic scene. But as one historian says, his "most immediate, and most influential 'source' . . . is, the repertory company of Victories, Glories, and *Patries* [image of *La France*], all those winged creatures or earthbound deities who represented at once *La France*, Marianne, and the Nation."

Like the flapper, the Communist was detested. The Russian Revolution had just taken place, and the Left was suspect. Neighborhood bullies intimidated local residents whose politics were considered radical. Reading the Communist paper, *l'Humanité*, was risky in the 1920s.

The hunger for "order" that the French show in this decade is an old story. French culture has a yen for order, as if it were the other side of the *enragé* coin, the blood-curdling revolutions. The rituals of the Bourbon court are about nothing if not order: the *levée*, the *couchée*, who could stand, sit, kneel this way or that in the presence of the king. A French meal is an ordered affair. Watch a child confronted with a buffet in an ordinary cafeteria. She will carefully organize her first, second, and third courses and then eat each one fastidiously, and probably silently, focusing on her food. In French art, order shapes the harmonious landscapes of Poussin, the architectural still lives and landscapes of Cézanne, the cubism of Braque and Picasso, the machine forms of Ozenfant, Le Corbusier, and Léger. Or compare a French garden to an English one. "Ordered" is the only appropriate adjective.

Within that ordering, as in the only apparently cool abstractions of Mondrian, there is infinite possibility. Order can unleash the imagination, or it can do the opposite; it can enforce strict limitation, or encourage infinite possibility. This is how Freud figured the fact and effect of the unconscious on people's lives. One was strictly limited by one's history, but within these limits, one could do anything.

In France in the 1920s, the French accumulated the foundation they needed to build a fascist state. Order, nationalism, celebration of the past, revival of Catholicism and the military, anti-Communism. All they needed was a scapegoat, and they found it in the Jews. The popularity of the *Comité de l'Action française*, a xenophobic, anti-Republican organization, soared. Their magazine, *Action française*, as one historian put it, "acquired an astonishing domination. . . . [It was] widely read in Catholic seminaries, where anti-Semitic racialism in which it specialized was appreciated."

The intolerance that conservative Catholic organizations nourished was, curiously, particularly virulent toward Jewish artists. Perhaps it's not curious, though, since art is so central to French patrimony and pride. Little did these proto-fascists know that they would be ruining French art for decades to come by their viciousness.

It became a habit to refer to people like Modigliani, Chagall, Soutine, Mané-Katz, Pascin, Orloff, and Marcoussis as the *Ecole de Paris* as opposed to the *Ecole français*. I always found these rubrics baffling and assumed there was some confusion at the time and that both were used for generally the same thing. I was wrong. *Ecole de Paris* was meant to designate foreign, primarily Jewish, artists. *Ecole français*, pure French artists.

In fact, the 1920s is a fascinating period in French art primarily because of the presence of those foreign artists. The collection of Paul Guillaume, amassed primarily in that decade and hanging today in the newly refurbished Orangerie in Paris, testifies to their talent. Nevertheless, many French critics and artists did not agree with Guillaume. During World War I, the painter Robert Delaunay wrote to a friend, "I am delighted with what you say . . . this stupid painting which was made by certain mystifiers who, for the most part, were foreigners to France, but who fooled the world by saying 'made in Paris' . . . I am happy to see that there are men . . . who have not allowed themselves to be invaded by this rot." He was talking about cubism and Picasso, who later would be confounded with Jews in art criticism.

Overtly racist language was saved for Jewish artists. On July 15, 1925, the respected magazine *Le Mercure de France* published an article by Fritz Vanderpyl titled "Is There Such a Thing as Jewish Painting?" He answered, "In the absence of any trace of Jewish art in the Louvre . . . we are nevertheless witnessing a swarming of Jewish painters." He then listed a string of artists with the name "Lévy." He continued, "To say nothing of the Lévys who prefer to exhibit under pseudonyms of less Jewish consonance, a move that would be quite in line with the ways of modern Jews, and without mentioning the Kohns, the Blochs, the Weills, . . ."

The painter Marcel Gromaire wrote in his diary in the early 1930s, "Here come the holidays. Paris rids itself of its whores, its pederasts, its eccentrics of all arts, its swarthy aliens who speak about 'their' France. . . ." He referred to the "destructive spirit of the Jews." Whores. Pederasts. Swarthy aliens. My, my, my.

Montparnasse was said to be "swarming" with Jewish artists. Louis Vauxcelles (himself a Jew, born Louis Meyer) deplored the Jewish inhabitants of the area: "It isn't a question of chauvinist politics . . . it is a simple matter of hygiene, of sanitation. . . ." Claude Roger-Marx (another Jew) wrote, "A barbarian horde has rushed like a plague, like a cloud of locusts, upon Montparnasse. . . . These are people from 'somewhere else' who know nothing of . . . the nuanced quality of our race. . . ." Waldemar George, a critic (and a Jew born Georges Jarocinsky), asked, "Does one detect . . . the *enjuivement* [Jewing] of contemporary Europe?" And Adolphe Basler (also a Jew!), a dealer and critic, described Chagall as a "folkloristic image maker . . . [who] unites the wilderness of the *moujik* [Russian peasant] and the madness of the young Jew who has damaged his brains by reading too much Talmud." The Jewish self-hatred is sickening, as is the desperation to be "French," to be an *Israélite*, an assimilated French Jew, and definitely not "Jewish" as in "Eastern European."

But it was the writer Camille Mauclair—not a Jew—who was the most influential. Mauclair published in places Jews could not, no matter how assimilated they thought they were. He wrote for the respected daily *Le Figaro* and for *l'Ami du People*, a weekly with a high circulation. "Montparnasse, inhabited as it was by eighty percent Semites," he wrote, "and every one of them a loser, served as the breeding ground for all ills in France." (Whoever thought artists could be so important?) Mauclair's articles were collected, in 1929 and 1930, into two volumes whose purpose was to isolate and mock the foreign artists who were ruining the greatness (and purity) of French art. The books' titles are *La Farce de l'art vivant: une campagne picturale 1928–1929* (The Farce of Art Today: Pictorial Warfare) and *Les Métèques contre l'art français* (Distasteful Foreigners Attack French Art). The first volume was a bestseller.

The germ-infested vocabulary—dirty, swarming, locusts, breeding ground, plague—is typical of anti-Semitic slurs. I remember the sign at the hotel near our house in Hurleyville: NO DOGS OR JEWS ALLOWED. Romy Golan's book *Modernity and Nostalgia* is the first to expose the extent of anti-Semitism in French culture in the 1920s. It is a brave and heartbreaking exposé. It strikes me that only a Jewish Israeli would have had the critical and emotional distance to write such a book.

—

So, in the popular lexicon of 1920s France, Picasso's cubism was no good, and neither was the expressionism of Chagall and Soutine, or the mannered neoclassicism of Modigliani, or the elegant cubism of Orloff. A kind of benign classicism became the style of the day. Picasso, Braque and Derain, Léger, Ozenfant and Le Corbusier all used some form of it. Artists who had been working abstractly, or nearly so, before the war often abandoned that style entirely. Landscapes, and landscapes with peasants, were highly salable. The *paysan* was god. "In the darkest hours, it is the French peasant's serene and determined gaze that has sustained my faith," said the hero of Verdun, General Pétain, who later became infamous for taking France into the Nazi camp. A person is *raciné*, rooted, in the French soil, or *déraciné*, not from here and not one of us. These terms were originated by the writer Maurice Barrès, the extreme nationalist and close friend of Charles Maurras, founder of the *Action française*. Foreign artists, including Picasso, were *déraciné*.

Most of the then-popular landscape painting by Derain,

Vlaminck, de Segonzac, de la Fresnaye, Metzinger, and lesser-known artists is forgotten today. It exhibited a simplified, even childlike, realism resonating with echoes of the past that instantly evoke longing. The pictures were dead, filled with what would not be faced: the dying, the loss of a generation, the fear of modernity, the fear of Germany and the United States. The fear of the future.

The popularity of Maurice Utrillo, son of Suzanne Valadon, is a telling example. His cityscapes are affectless and obvious. They give us flattened views of whitewashed, purified Montmartre streets. By the late 1920s, Utrillo's sales were soaring while the provocatively original paintings by his mother were languishing. One critic put it aptly, "Utrillo's work depicts the resurgence of an almost abolished world. . . . It is the immobile world of outdated architecture which preceded the war. . . . A world both obsolete and calm . . . a world which orders itself entirely around the church and the small village hall."

Valadon, meanwhile, was making paintings of willful women, naked or dressed, including a stark self-portrait where she is nude to the waist and staring coldly out at the viewer. No charming mother-type, she. There is also a picture of a large woman in brashly striped trousers smoking in bed, and another in a fire-engine-red dress seated in an armchair with her stockings rolled down, the very picture of insouciance. These women were *not* Coco Chanel's ideal type, but neither were they doting mothers or churchgoers. They were ordinary working-class women.

France was furiously not looking at itself and its problems. As is its wont, it blamed someone else. So, in the most culturally varied period of its history, it became the most xenophobic and hostile to outside influences. Communism and Jews became the enemy. A popular slogan in the late Thirties was "Better Hitler than [the Jew and socialist] Blum" as Prime Minister.

———

The Twenties could have been a period of extraordinary adventure culturally, politically, and economically. So much was changing in the world—there were cars and airplanes, jazz and short skirts, bobbed hair and skyscrapers, socialism. The French might have welcomed the foreigners who poured into their country from southern and eastern Europe looking for work and escaping oppression. They took them into their workforce—they had to, considering the numbers of French men who had died in the war—but not really into their country. Or, to be more precise, the more French you looked—say, Portuguese or Italian—and the more willing you were to put aside your origins, the easier it would be to become French. Today, there are no Muslims in major political offices in France, and only one who heads a large company. Only in 2006 did a Muslim become an important commentator on TV. Nor do we see the work of people of color in art galleries, or on bookstore shelves. I guess they don't look French.

Immigrants modernize a country by exposing its citizens to other languages and food, new ways of thinking, other styles of dress, gesturing, behaving. But modernity was not what a large segment of the French population wanted in the twenties. Not economically, not socially, not culturally. What they were concerned with was their history and their patrimony. Their Glory. The severe damaging of Reims cathedral in the north, where French kings had been crowned since the early ninth century, became the mightiest of symbols. The contemporary writer Romain Rolland put it this way: "Our France which bleeds with so many wounds has suffered nothing more cruel than the attack against her Parthenon, the Cathedral of Reims, 'Our Lady of France.'" This is a shocking statement, when you think about the millions dead and maimed, the bereft parents and children, brothers and sisters, friends and lovers.

Why did the French turn to their history to heal themselves? Why not to the present and future, a new world? This turning to the past, where glorious France resides and will save them, reminds me of France after the riots and car burnings in the *banlieues* in November 2005. They repeat their republican mantra, "We are all French; we are all equal." They say this in the face of their blatant racism toward Arabs and African blacks who are French citizens, and who are unemployed or have the most menial jobs and who live in high-rise ghettos far from postcard-perfect Paris. The French response to World War I, their withdrawal into the past and their hatred of outsiders, doomed them to this blindness, to this heartlessness.

French dislike of outsiders in the Twenties ironically tossed them up onto fascist shores and toward the Germans, whom they had despised for over a century. By 1940, the French saluted their former enemies, and rounded up Jews and Communists, homosexuals and Gypsies. Then, a decade later, they killed and tortured Algerians. And today they turn a blind eye to their "foreign" populations in the suburbs. It was the Glory of France, *la France Éternelle*, nationalism, that suckered them in the Twenties and still holds them in thrall today.

Why didn't the French think about what brought them to such a war, and why they hadn't tried to stop it before so many died so uselessly? No, they would rather cling to their symbols, their fears, and their hatred. Whatever France did was best. Germany in the Twenties might have been growing ever more powerful and modern, but France was the true country of culture, the French felt. France knew where the real values were, in the peasants and in the land, in the church and the military. This, along with their anti-Semitism, shaped future decades. You could call it fear. The manager of a magnificent thirteenth-century convent-turned-hotel, where I finished this book, called it that. He asked: "Have you noticed how the French always say *'Non'* before they can get anywhere near *'Oui'*? We are afraid of everything we don't know and everyone who is not like us."

It was as hard to remake a life in France after the war as it was to remake a face. Those recomposed faces that Hemingway saw everywhere he went in Paris were like the French in general, reconstructed cosmetically but not fundamentally. Death and destruction sent the French into trauma. Then they crippled their souls with their "Frenchness."

Here, then, are two unequal impulses of the Twenties. On the one hand, to let it all out, dance your heart away, mingle with blacks and gays, live a wild life, eat foreign foods, fantasize about America. On the other hand, to hold everything in tight, to keep the ugliness so far away that you might not even know it is there, to calm yourself with nostalgia and hatred of Others. Today in France they're holding it in again. There is no interesting art or literature to speak of, and they ignore at their peril a huge immigrant population in just the way the aristocracy ignored the Third Estate in the late eighteenth century. We all know what happened then.

I feel terribly sorry about French suffering in World War I, but I do not forgive them for what they have not learned. There is no glory in it.

CHAPTER 5

Flight

W hat is Paris the capital of today?
It's true that the most ordinary eating in France is
still superior to anywhere else. If you want the greatest hot
chocolate in the world, you must go to Angelina's on the rue de
Rivoli. Haircuts look better here too. But Milan does a fine job.
And so do Berlin and Tokyo. You don't have to come to Paris
to buy Chanel or Dior or Yves St. Laurent. You certainly don't
have to come for art. Except for old art. But if you want the
adventure of the contemporary, what Man Ray was looking for
in the 1920s and Mary Cassatt fifty years earlier, you won't find
it in Paris. Young artists don't pop out of art school in Los
Angeles or New York, look at each other, and say "Hey, let's go
to Paris!"

So what am I doing here? Art is at the very center of my life. I know what a terrific sublimator I am. I remember that painting of *The Doctor* in my grandparents' kitchen all those years ago. How I fled the loneliness around the table that winter's day and slipped into the picture with the parents and their dying child. And now I live in a country where art is yesterday, both the world of curated historical exhibitions and contemporary art. My acquaintance, the hotel director in the south of France, tells me, "France has become a kind of Disneyland." His own inn, the Gothic convent with its thirteenth-century cloister, is used primarily as a set for grandiose weddings.

While staying at the convent, I was invited for a drink in a little town nearby. I sat on a terrace overlooking the vineyards and mountains of La Sainte-Baume, not far from Aix. I sipped aperitifs with two retired physical therapists in the February sun by their pool, and one of them said to me, "I hope you will be here in April and we will go to Les Baux together. There are huge caves there where they do wonderful shows. Last year they projected the great cathedrals of France in the caves, and this year it will be Cézanne."

Or, as Marx commented about history repeating itself, "the first time as tragedy, the second as farce."

Maybe France's time is over. Empires, countries, cities, come and go. Where is Babylon or Knossos, Athens or Sparta? Rome, Florence, or El Dorado? We have seen countries disappear from maps of great civilizations, Babylonia and Egypt first of all. Still, it feels glib to doom France, a country of such natural and creative wealth and such prestige. Not to mention that it's my home and I'm happy here.

Ken made a painting some years ago of a charging caval-
ryman after a picture by Théodore Géricault. The text read:
"How accepting can you be without becoming complacent?" Is
that France's problem?

The French are neither proud nor certain of much today. In
the spring of 2005, Jacques Chirac, the center-right president,
campaigned intensely for a "Yes" vote on the European constitution, and the country resoundingly said "No." It is not clear
what the "No" meant, and people, sullen and confused the next
day, were not proud of themselves. Was it "No" to all the immigrants in France, plus the high unemployment rate? "No" to
English- and American-style capitalism, with its reduced state
support for health care, unemployment insurance, daycare,
retirement pensions—and a definite "No" to their meager
vacations? Or was it "No" to the bureaucrats in Brussels, who
run the European show, haughtily ignoring their national con-
stituencies?

Right after this vote, Paris lost its bid for the Olympic
Games of 2012. They had made a visible effort to win these,
unusual behavior for the normally cool French. They deco-
rated Paris gaily with inverted cones of blue, violet, green, red,
and yellow neon rings and jaunty posters with the logo connecting the "s" in Paris with the "2" in 2012 to form a heart: "I
love Paris. . . ." Oh, the poor Parisians waiting for the decision,
hovering around the plaza outside the Hotel de Ville, staring
longingly up at the huge screen where the announcement
would appear.

A few days earlier, Chirac had boasted: Never London. It's not possible. You can't eat there. The French did scorn him the day London won. Even presidents have lost their prestige in France. Who would have sneered at de Gaulle, Pompidou, Giscard d'Estaing, or Mitterrand?

The French got another chance in the World Cup competitions in July 2006. Unexpectedly, they came within an inch of beating the Italians in the final match. But then, seemingly out of the blue, the fierce and graceful Zinedine Zidane—called Zizou by his fans—head-butted the Italian player Marco Materazzi and was thrown out of the game. Later, Zidane said the Italian had slurred his mother and sister. His family said that a racist comment was made. The French lost the match.

Unemployment is sky-high. Youths in segregated suburbs are morose. It was these young men, mostly second- and third-generation French children of North African immigrants, who flew into a rage in November 2005 after two kids fleeing police accidentally electrocuted themselves on a live wire. Cars and small businesses burned in cities all over France for weeks. Miraculously, only one other person died.

At the *rentrée* of 2005, the "re-entry" to normal life after summer, people responded sourly to survey questions. Only 30 percent said they were optimistic about their future. A year earlier, it had been 59 percent. The figure slipped to 26 percent when they were asked about their hopefulness addressing questions of poverty, and it fell a little lower still, to 25 percent, concerning unemployment and the loss of production and jobs to other countries. Only 14 percent of the French were optimistic about having enough money to buy what they want.

Since the November 2005 riots, the government has tried to figure out what to do. One friend said to me it's been bound to happen for thirty years. She was referring to the economic crisis that hit France in the mid-1970s, when the price of oil rose dramatically and thousands of North African immigrants lost their jobs but stayed in France. Assimilating these immigrants was distasteful to the French. It is at such moments that they turn nasty. They are not good at sharing, and they are excellent at blaming.

The government was jolted again when millions of students filled the streets of French cities in March and April 2006, merrily, sometimes aggressively demanding repeal of a labor law that could fire them without explanation during a two-year period until the age of twenty-six. Before the strike reached the proportions of 1968, which it was fast approaching, the government backed down.

Still, it's calming to live in France if you're an American. Daily life, like a lullaby, is soothing. Things go along the way they always have, with a certain graciousness and elegance. It may take ages to get anything fixed, but it ultimately happens. And you are obliged to have long conversations with your concierge, even if you'd rather throw out the garbage and go straight back to your desk. You go out to dinner at your favorite wine bar and enjoy the perfect preparation of your meal as well as the service, and unless you're in a hurry, you'll savor its leisurely pace, complete with a cordial chat with the owners. You get used to it; you acknowledge the civility of this behavior, that it does something good for you. But it is a little slow in Paris.

This leisurely, almost aimless pace, like the wanderings of

Monica Vitti in an Antonioni movie, hits you when you visit London. Until I moved to Paris and began visiting often, I took the English capital to be Old London, like the British Museum, the Strand or Piccadilly Circus. I remembered its dark, block-long buildings, still a bit Dickensian here and there, if starkly neoclassically white elsewhere. London, I thought, is pre-dictable and boring. But no more.

The city may be only 212 miles away from Paris, two and a half hours on the train, but the differences feel generational, even geographic, as in this side of the Atlantic or the other. You disembark in London and, rain or shine, hot or cold, the first thing that strikes you is the energy of the place, people rushing—open-faced and clean-shaven, square of jaw and body—on the march in their dowdy clothing, piling into their lives. It's gritty and blowy; ambition is in the air. You want to get somewhere, although you're not sure where, and it is just that uncertainty that is the adventure.

At first I'm not aware of the pleasures that slip away in the rush. But then I notice that I can't find a decent cup of coffee except at Starbuck's. There's one opposite the British Museum, so you can mosey across the street and linger at the horsemen on the Parthenon frieze with their fine limbs and delicately clinging garments. Or admire the seated gods leaning into each other in rapt conversation. And if you stay for a while, why, you can slide right back into those old, slow Paris pleasures.

Still, the Gallic capital is downright shabby and indolent by comparison, if also perfumed and charming. Max Weber got it right. Capitalism does work better in Protestant countries. But certainly it can't be capitalism alone that makes a nation exciting. France always lagged behind England, Germany, and

America in terms of industrial development, their political revolution inspiring them more than economic ingenuity. Yet
Paris has only recently become noticeably less interesting.
Does it want to trail its long skirts, high heels, and sexy
unmade-bed haircuts while its neighbors fly by on their
scooters, with lower unemployment, higher production,
greater purchasing power, *and* great contemporary art? (At
least the food is still lousy in London.)

The French certainly don't want to be like the British or the
Americans. Political differences among the French evaporate
in their shared abhorrence of the liberal economics of Anglo-
Saxon countries. Not to mention their condescension toward
their taste. The French treasure their orchards and vineyards,
their Bresse chickens and Charolais cows. And many would
like to linger in their past and make all the foreigners go away.
Then, they think, employment will go up, and maybe they
could also toss those annoying computers. Many really don't
want to be bothered by the latest technology and irritating
social problems. They want their old good life back. Nonethe-
less, they are suffering from the kind of malaise the English
showed as their empire evaporated. The French cannot bear
the idea that they've become a second-class country, so they
cast their glances back again to "Eternal France." But where
exactly is that France?

———

Today, more and more, Parisians are barging into each other
angrily without apology. If you ask the proprietor of your bar next
door to please talk more softly in the street in front of your

windows at 3 A.M. and please stop blasting music illegally night
and day, he screams, "You're only saying that to me because
I'm Arab." I thought he was French. People defiantly hang their
most intimate linen along their balconies, even in middle-class
neighborhoods, a kind of "Fuck you" to their neighbors. Others
scream at each other across courtyards to lower their TVs and
stereos, and voices. Noise pollution is a steady topic of media
attention, accompanied by giant images of gaping-mouthed
shrieking Parisians. Large cities are like this, of course, but
Paris never used to be. Paris was a civil, soft-spoken place. You
might have sensed anger beneath the surface, the anger that
you knew erupted periodically in riots and revolution, but, still,
you expected politeness and calm. No longer.

Car drivers complain about bike riders, and vice versa.
Refurbished and reduced driving lanes for cars with specific
allotments for buses, taxis, and bikes, dramatically cutting air
pollution, get hardly any appreciation. Instead, people complain endlessly about the numbers of children "certain people"
are having with *more* than one wife, and how much unemployment insurance "they" are collecting while they work under
the table at the same time, and how *our* taxes take care of *their*
families. The accused begin to cry Enough! and the suburbs go
up in flames.

The French can't understand what's happened. They used to
have the best country in the world. Now you can't get a DSL
line installed in less than three weeks or a new chip for your
cell phone in less than two. They never noticed things like this
before or cared, but now they know it's faster in London or the
United States or Germany. Or India! France is falling behind.
The kids know it more than anyone else. They see the world

they want to be part of on TV and in films. They are dying to try out their movie-drenched English. Popular songs are the lingua franca of young people everywhere—and the good ones aren't made in France. The language is English, everywhere.

French politics, too, are in a shambles. Historically a beacon of democracy, the founder of revolutionary liberty, the French now vote increasingly for the fascist National Front led by Jean-Marie Le Pen. They did this before, most horrifically in the 1930s. And for similar reasons, foremost among them the desire for national purity. Le Pen's political ideology is utterly race-based: Immigrants are ruining divine France. He rallies his audiences with paeans to Marshal Pétain, Joan of Arc, French Algeria: France for the French.

President Chirac looks worse and worse, his paunchy face dragging his sagging body and corrupt spirit around. Politicians have grown more conservative and racist, as the youngish Interior Minister (and possible next president) Nicolas Sarkozy imitates Le Pen and Prime Minister Dominique de Villepin (Chirac's man) imitates Sarkozy. They are looking for the middle of the road, as England did with Blair and the United States did with Clinton. They all lean rightward, like the Germans did in their election of Angela Merkel as president in 2005.

The French don't know where to turn. Their behavior is defensive. They hope they are still the proud French, but they are not. They are scared and stumbling. A stinging reminder of their national misery is the state of the arts. Their formerly radiant art and literature are moribund. Only film still amazes on a world scale. The French could be using their arts to ask important questions, but they have lost the habit of bravery.

Instead, they are riveted by the growing population of Others in their midst. Their sense of themselves and their country has turned into a science fiction scenario of endlessly reproducing humanoids who bear no resemblance to themselves.

For a couple of years, I tried to ignore the miserable situation in France as I hacked away at my father and his brother in my doomed book about the two of them. Over and over again, my father stepped forward as the betrayer. My dancey dad wriggled out of every commitment: "I can't walk with Mom on the street; she's pregnant and looks ugly." "Oh, I'm sorry, Eunie, I can't make it to your wedding, I fell." "No, I didn't give my parents Dave's letters. It slipped my mind."

Before his brother went to Spain, he said to him: "I can't go, I'm a married man." But that's not why he didn't go. How often my father repeated, "I'm not afraid to die. It's normal, everybody dies." Over and over again he said this: "I'm not afraid." How it must have tormented him, that it was his sweet brother who was going to be the tough guy, the warrior. "I've seen plenty in my life, believe me," said my dad. "Dying doesn't scare me." But he was lying, something he always did. He was afraid to go to Spain. He was afraid to die. It turns out that he lied to me about France, too.

———

Until the 1990s, there were extraordinary historical exhibitions to see in Paris. I would come in from the airport, drop off my bags and rush out to the Grand Palais. Now I go look at designer boutiques at Galeries Lafayette. One of the last great exhibits, in 1991, was of Théodore Géricault, that odd nineteenth-century romantic painter. Many people remember Géricault's spectacular *Raft of the Medusa* in the Louvre's Great Hall; others know his unnerving portraits of the insane; a few, his strange landscapes. But this show displayed a startling number of taut, magnificent horses with shiny rumps and silken tails. It was a sly show of tails and asses.

In the late 1990s and early 2000s, museum shows of great interest vanished. All you found were dreary monographic installations of the work of Gauguin, Constable, Signac, and Poussin. Or of twentieth-century artists like Rouault, Jean Hélion, Nicholas de Stäel, and Francis Picabia. Or group shows like the Origins of Impressionism or Egyptian Art from the Time of the Pyramids. All of it miserably boring. Only the Jeu de Paume and the Cartier Foundation disturbed the abiding ennui from time to time.

I couldn't but notice what was happening in the French art world, and I was dreadfully disappointed. It was obvious that there was nothing in Paris that could compete with London. London! No one put London and art together. London was a literary town. Okay, Gainsborough, Turner, and Constable, Francis Bacon and Lucian Freud. But Paris was where you were supposed to go to use your eyes, and then your mind and your heart, and yes, your body.

But it was in London, at the new Tate Modern, located in a former power station, where the straitjacket of chronology was chucked and the permanent collection danced thematically across the museum's floors. Then there was the smashing private collection of Charles Saatchi. And competitions of contemporary art, like the one for the prestigious Turner Prize, were installed in historic fine-arts museums like the Tate Britain, with its eighteenth- and nineteenth-century British collections. Even the hoary British Museum, bullhorn in hand, pulled the public in with contemporary art. Particularly wonderful in late 2002 was *Field for the British Isles* by Antony Gormley. Filling the floor of a gallery that one could only peer into were thousands of little terra-cotta pieces, looking like midget un-gods. It was a modern-day grouping of Sumerian idols, the sources of which were in a room nearby. This exhibit made you think about the ancient and present Middle East and its relationship to the West. It brought you to politics and pounding contemporary issues. It felt important.

The art world—curated historic shows and contemporary art—in London somersaulted like a kid on the beach, a kind of highbrow, high-stepping Billy Elliott. It was charming and loud, seductive and upsetting. Museums and galleries were packed. Crowds were lively. Bets were placed on who would win the Turner Prize! How very dreary next-door Paris looked—with its uninteresting historic exhibitions, its dull gallery scene, and so few important collectors.

In the early 1990s, the YBAs—Young British Artists—burst on the scene, and with them their collector, Charles Saatchi, who bought both international and British contemporary art in quantity. He acquired hair-raising works. Many were inspired by postmodern technologies like video cameras and computers, as well as photography. They shredded old molds. Painting would not do for them. Not as it had been, anyway.

The YBAs worked big and with enormous chutzpah. They pulled their material, psychological and physical, from their hollering, gross childhoods, lugubrious curiosities, ethnic heritages. Double-life-size photographs of drunken parents vomiting into toilet bowls amidst the comparable mayhem of their apartments. Cows cut dead in half to expose the intricacy—and beauty?—of their innards, standing abjectly tethered in colossal tanks of formaldehyde. A sculptor turned furniture and buildings inside out, where they mutely oozed the meaning of what they weren't, and wouldn't be. Old Master paintings inflated into sculptures where figures wore dresses and suits made from bright African print cloth. The Virgin Mary cloaked in star-studded midnight blue with elephant dung stuck to the surface, creating a halo for today. The artists came from the working classes and were often women. Frequently they were immigrants of different colors and backgrounds. The face of British contemporary art was like the face of Britain, outrageous and inspiring.

Parenthetically, some say that London was selected to host the 2012 Olympic Games because in their publicity and presentations in Singapore, where the decision was being made, the British emphasized the multicultural character of London. They also brought with them thirty children who spoke twenty-eight different languages. Given the recent racially motivated riots in France, this was a shrewd strategy.

If London, out of nowhere, could produce a hot art world and art market, you would think Paris could change, too. Really—England and art? This was not a small change. Landmasses moved. Something similar is happening in India and China today, as exciting art pours out of these countries. These developments are not simply due to the economic booms in each country. Rather, they are born from conflicts, the tensions produced by social, political, and economic movement. Ideas and emotions are molten. France, by contrast, is stuck, strangled by its good taste, choking on undigested pieces of its history. Something prevents it from arguing and playing, ripping up the past and moving on. What I wouldn't give to see some irreverence in French art. And some courage.

—

On June 11, 2005, *Le Monde* published an article bemoaning the almost total absence of French artists at the Venice Biennale, the important international exhibition that was about to open. It contained only one French artist out of ninety-one. In contemporary exhibits all over the city timed to accompany the Biennale, there were only four French artists. It was also noted in the article that in the recent reopening of the New York Museum of Modern Art in November 2004, only one living French artist was included.

Le Monde asked an international group of curators, gallerists, museum directors, and collectors why they thought this was the case. One of the organizers of the Biennale said flatly, "I didn't find artists in France who interested me." An influential dealer in Zurich agreed, "We haven't found the French interesting these last few years." Many pointed to the fact that French artists traveled little, particularly to the United States, "a country of big collectors, galleries, and auction houses." "The French," responded an art dealer from Berlin, "are closed in on themselves." Another dealer suggested that the French state buys up its artists' work but immediately stores it in depots. The work plays no part in contemporary dialogue. A museum director in Barcelona rhetorically asked the *Le Monde* reporter, "Why do American and German artists dominate today?" And answered, "Because their economies and their collectors are dominant." The last sentence in the article was this: "Cities play a very important role in art. Now Paris has lost her place as a center of innovation. Moscow and London are much more international." Paris is yesterday.

One of the interviewees suggested that the French economy has dried up and that that's the problem. Another said the state takes too good care of artists, so they have no drive. Certainly there is an underlying antagonism in Europe and the United States toward the French welfare state. The very word "welfare" has such a dreary, loser ring to it. But faring well cannot be a bad thing in itself. In my opinion, France's problems come from elsewhere.

Why is an esthetic of violence, pain, irony, and rage so alien to their artistic sensibility? It is certainly not alien to their culture and history. And why is it that French artists can't be any color but white? Or rather, that artists of color can make art, but no one will care?

Museum curators in Paris don't go out to the city's suburbs, where the most interesting exhibits of contemporary art take place at centers in Ivry, Fresnes, Juvizy, Brétigny. Is this because the populations of many of these suburbs are not of European French background? Are the curators indifferent? lazy? ruined by their state-appointed jobs, which they hold for life? Or are they afraid? Afraid of people of different races? Afraid of what they'll see there? Afraid they'll want to change?

In 2001, Régis Michel, the director of the Department of Graphic Arts at the Louvre, mounted the unforgettable exhibition "Painting as Crime." It was he who, ten years earlier, had curated the Géricault show. At the beginning and end of "Painting as Crime" hung larger-than-lifesize black-and-white photographs of the entrance to Auschwitz. This is not a scene the French are interested in looking at. They continue to avoid Marcel Ophuls's 1971 film, *The Sorrow and the Pity*, which exposed for the first time, and in extensive and irrefutable detail, the French collaboration with the Nazis. Michel's exhibit was a critique of modernist art and included painting, photography, and video. You walked through dramatically lighted spaces, rooms, antechambers, and corridors confronted with a heady mix of Marxist assumptions about power and ideology and Lacanian concepts of Self and Other. It was not a show to "enjoy." Nor was it beautiful. It did not care about art as pleasure in the old French sense of pretty and amusing. But it gave you a lot to think about. It made you wonder about "beauty." *Whose* beauty? Why? It forced you to think about art's moral responsibilities. At the same time as you wandered the spaces, you traveled the rails on the outskirts of modern art, its fears and trepidations, its desires and disappointments. Not many Parisians saw the exhibit. The problem was, it wasn't very French.

⌒

France's distaste for Others and her need for conventional beauty and good taste put her into a most peculiar relationship with the most famous foreign artist who had lived in

Pablo Picasso, *Demoiselles d'Avignon*, 1907, Museum of Modern Art, New York

France since Leonardo da Vinci. Despite his fame, Pablo Picasso was never really welcome.

In 1907, at twenty-six years old, he made a shocking painting that measured approximately eight by eight feet. He called it the *Demoiselles d'Avignon*. Five large female figures resembling pre-Roman Iberian sculpture, French Congo and Ivory Coast carvings, and Egyptian wall painting stare the viewer down. The women flaunt their bodies with the confidence of fertility gods. Shameless and ugly, these girls are not French.

The job of a female nude is to be beautiful, desirable, possessible. Think of Renoir, Matisse, later Bonnard (but not De Kooning, whose women are direct descendants of Picasso's

Demoiselles). The painter Andre Derain is supposed to have said about this canvas, "One day we will find that Picasso has hanged himself behind this painting." But, as an art historian wittily noted, "it was the picture that to a certain extent hanged Derain," whose measured, harmonious classicism instantly wilted by comparison. The *Demoiselles* sent Beauty packing.

It has become clear over the years that the twentieth century was no place for representations of Beauty—or of Love, for that matter. A century where millions died in ditches and ovens, where torture was condoned by civilized countries, where genocide occurred over and over again. It was the ironic, questioning, and obsessive meditations of Proust, Virginia Woolf, Heinrich Boll, Pat Barker, Philip Roth, Marcel Duchamp, Warhol, and Cindy Sherman that provided the right gloss on the century. But not, it turns out, for France. The French didn't have the stomach for it. They would stick to beauty.

Picasso remained an interloper. Small, dark, intense, and Spanish-speaking, he was also overtly ambitious and competitive, qualities that were not French. He was always and insistently Other, and he acted as if he had a right to whatever he wanted. French xenophobia didn't touch him. The French never liked him, they just accepted him as their due, as his worldly fame redounded to them. When anti-Semitic obscenities became commonplace in the Twenties, art critics tossed Picasso in with the Jews and the homosexuals. If only France could have embraced Picasso. If only.

In 2003, I begin to write in a café on the Boulevard Magenta near the Gare de l'Est. It is a simple, pared-down place whose major business is in coffee and beer. The clientele is largely French men of Algerian descent. If you ask for a sandwich, the guy behind the bar suggests that you go across the street to the bakery and bring one back. I like the café because I can go there any time of day or night and work. It is often noisy, both from a large portable radio–CD player and from a television that is always on, but you get used to it.

One day, a depressed and angry woman in her early thirties starts working behind the bar. She hears me speaking English to someone and indicates later in the afternoon that she speaks English too. Occasionally we chat. Her name is Rachel. Her family is from Oran and she is Muslim. One day I ask her how she happens to have a Jewish name. She says, "My mother's best friend in Algiers was Jewish. She named me after her."

Later that week, there's a demonstration near the bar. It's made up of black Africans. Rachel is irritated. I ask her why, and she says, "They just come here and become French citizens and the government gives them opportunities we never get and they still complain. When I was in high school, I challenged my history professor to teach the Algerian War. I got a blank stare. What war, she said. I corrected stupid prejudices about Islam. I told them how cleanliness is taught by the Koran, and that they should know how important personal hygiene is to Muslims. Again blank stares."

Her teachers really didn't know what she was talking about. Until 1999, the French did not acknowledge that there had been a war in Algeria. It was the war that didn't speak its name. In French minds, Algeria had been part of France and no longer was. They claimed that Algerians had benefited from Republican ideals, and that they were considered French. They had the same opportunities as everybody else. So whatever happened to them when they moved to mainland France was their own problem.

In fact, Muslim Algerians and their particular history were invisible to French people. As a French historian put it, "That mysterious 'other' [in Algeria] had resisted, had wanted to obtain a nationality of his own; here was a man whose life, hopes, and history no one took the trouble to find out about. How very distant and strange the Aurès [a mountainous region in Algeria] and their inhabitants seemed to the French."

James Baldwin evoked the same distress describing his life in America. He wrote, "that to be a Negro meant, precisely, that one was never looked at but was simply at the mercy of the reflexes the color of one's skin caused in other people." He felt he'd contracted a "dread, chronic disease . . . [and that] once this disease is contracted, one can never be really carefree again, for the fever, without an instant's warning, can recur at any moment. . . . There is not a Negro alive who does not have this rage in his blood."

I sense this in Rachel. No matter what she does, she is Other and invisible. Her rage devours her. She is, as one expert on Algeria put it, "mutilated by oppression. . . ."

———

France became involved with Algeria in the 1830s. Unlike Morocco and Tunisia, which remained protectorates, Algeria, by the late nineteenth century, became three departments (or states) of France. It could be considered the southernmost part of the country. Born in Algeria to French parents, Albert Camus was against an independent Algeria, because he saw his country and southern mainland France as part of one Mediterranean culture. He deluded himself into thinking that France would allow native Algerians to be equal to the *pieds noirs,* the French who started moving there in the late nineteenth century. They thought they were building a French culture for the Muslim Algerians as well as for the French. But they were colonizers. They benefited from cheap Algerian labor.

Although from 1947 on some Algerians voted, it was not one person, one vote as it was for people of European French origin. Only an elite few Algerians were allowed to vote. They were considered by the French to be subjects, not citizens. On the Algerian side, many protected their Arab and Muslim identities and did not want to adjust their thinking and social practices to fit the French civil code. Ultimately, they wanted their own country, not the right to vote in "France."

Still, leftists in and out of the country, like Camus, thought they could work things out. They believed in the myth of a democratic France for all. One writer put it succinctly: "Leftists refused to admit that reconciliation was not possible. This was based on the simple truth that the liberals did not understand that once colonial exploitation was removed, Europeans would have no reason to remain in Algeria."

Camus was an idealist. His idealism is understandable, once you realize how thoroughly the notion of universality is at the heart of the French Revolution, French Republicanism, and French identity. The French simply cannot admit how badly they treated and used Algerians, and how they thought of them as inferior. It would give the lie to their whole polit-ical-philosophical infrastructure. What the French offered Algerians, they thought, was the opportunity to become French. And they were not even wholehearted or honest about that. What they *never* offered was the opportunity for Alge-rians to become French *and* keep their Algerian culture. Why, after all, would they want to—the European French person thought—when offered the possibility of French culture? Who in their right mind could possibly think that an Algerian would not want to exchange his inferior culture for the obviously superior French one?

The Algerian war lasted from 1954 until 1962. Most French people were shocked by what happened. They hadn't noticed Algeria, and when they did, they found Algerians savage and ungrateful. This vile war that sanctioned torture and violence ruined both countries. It marked the end of the myth of French universality. But the French don't seem to know that, even now. They are stubbornly attached to their Republican ideals, which, for many, exist in name only. They are blind to their racism, and it is as crippling to them as their distortion of their history and the heritage from both world wars.

The French-born rap star Monsieur R (Richard Makela), whose parents are Congolese immigrants and who grew up in a housing project outside Paris, sings, "France abandoned its children without warning. Like my Jewish brothers controlled by Nazis. Now it's France that checks my color. So understand my hate. I'm in pain." The name of the song is "FranSSe," with an obvious reference to the Nazi SS.

The French have been using the crutch of their exceptionalism, their great Revolution, for too long. They are terrified of facing who they are, that they are neither the upholder of great democratic values, nor, any longer, the producer of cultural genius. They trudge around in the same circles, wearing themselves down into the rut where they now stand, which is nearly below eye level. They have good reason to be scared. Who are they indeed?

⁓

At bottom, I think the French can't stand Rachel's square face and features, which look thick compared to many French people of European background. They don't like her kinky hair and thick, peasant-like body. One writer points to "the readiness of state commissions before, during and after the Second World War to rate immigrants in terms of their potential to be 'assimilated.' Those from North Africa always came last." Undoubtedly, the Algerian "look" is intertwined in French eyes with their miserable history together.

For centuries, Jewish noses were too large, foreheads too low, lips too full. A priest during World War II asked one of his parishioners, "My friend, do you know that God created man in his image, and do you know what that meant?". . . "I do understand [the parishioner answered], I have seen the Marshal." He was referring to Pétain's blue eyes and snowy white moustache, physical characteristics the governmentally controlled press repeated endlessly. In time, prejudice against a certain kind of Jewish look faded. Now the facial type of the Jews they killed, the Ashkenazi Jews, is seen as European, while it is Sephardic Jews and Algerians who are unattractive.

Paul Morand, a popular writer of the Twenties and early Thirties who obsessed about overbearing women and lesbians, also detested foreigners. France is sick, he wrote, with "periodic eczema of Italian emigration; suspect spots of Romanian origin; colonies of American boils; Levantine pus." His contemporary and confrere Céline, who put his racial hatred to work for the Germans, wrote in 1934, "While the war [World War I] was still on, the seed of our hateful peace was being sown. A hysterical bitch, you could see her squinting out of a hundred mirrors, stamping her feet in the dust and despair to the music of a Negro-Judaeo-Saxon band."

Today, National Front politicians say things like the Holocaust is a "mere detail" of World War II, and Chirac is "in the pay of Jewish organizations." They declare that "the races are not equal . . . there are differences in the genes" and that "there are simply too many immigrants, and they make who knows how many children whom they send into the streets and then claim welfare." Send the immigrants "home."

In one of the strongest National Front centers, Provence, I encountered unabashed xenophobia regularly. When I bought my bread, the baker wanted to talk about how many children the "Arabs" are having with how many wives. The French really seem to think they are about to disappear, that any minute now it will be their turn to be invisible.

Monsieur R says, "First, officials blamed the riots on the practice of polygamy, which they claim leaves inordinate numbers of mothers to raise children on their own. Then, they blamed Islamic fundamentalists. Everyone got blamed except the elected officials, the ones who are supposed to ensure that everyone has liberty, fraternity, equality."

In that little southern town where I finished this book, a young gay couple fled the center of the village after their car was scratched several times with the words "Homo" and "Pédé." Fag. The French are sick with their hatred of Others. It's killing them.

———

Yes, I am haunted by my own Otherness in France. I am haunted by the Collaboration. I was born in 1941, and that is perhaps explanation enough. I now live in a country that would have sent me away. I would have waited like others did, seated on the edge of a bed, my coat on, my yellow Star of David stitched carefully in place. I'd clutch my mother's hand. We'd wait. And if I survived, I would grow up to be a repressed, polite French Ashkenazi Jew.

Jews were excluded from public office in October 1940. This was not ordered by the Germans; it was French-initiated. In the Occupied Zone with Paris at the center—its boundaries reaching down past Bordeaux to the Spanish border in the southwest, then up to Tours, down a bit to Bourges, up north again to Dijon, Reims, and Amiens in the east—Jews were required, starting in May 1942, to wear the Yellow Star on their outer clothing. In the unoccupied zone, Vichy France, generally the southern and southeastern part of the country including Lyon, Vienne, Avignon, Aix, and Marseille, Jewish passports were stamped *"Juif."*

Exclusion moved relentlessly toward murder. By the end of the war, more than 75,000 Jews had been rounded up in the dread *rafles*, deportations, a word that sounds like "Hitler" and

"Nazi" and "Gestapo" to Jewish ears. They were crushed into railway cars and sent to Poland to be asphyxiated or, if they were lucky, worked and starved to death. Of these 75,000, 2,567 survived. Twenty-five hundred and sixty seven. These are German statistics.

A recent historian describes the turning point for French Jews: "On 16 and 17 July 1942 some 9000 French police arrested 12,884 Jews and herded them into a sports stadium. . . . Over 7000, including 4000 children, were kept inside the stadium for five days, in insufferable heat . . . with little or no water and food, and no sanitation, the children forced into terrible squalor through dysentery and diarrhea. . . . The target for deportation had been twice as high as the numbers seized. Because of the shortfall, the youngest children, unwanted by the Germans . . . were finally sent to be deported from Drancy, seven-year-olds trailing their younger brothers or sisters by the hand in pitiful scenes of fear and distress."

The Vichy government substituted busts of Marshal Pétain for Marianne. The authoritarian Father took the place of the protective Mother.

The extremes of the 1930s are there to scare the wits out of me. First the French went far to the left with the Popular Front and their groundbreaking laws enforcing paid vacation, a minimum wage, unemployment insurance. Then they turned and bowed to the Nazis. "No other authority in Nazi-occupied Western Europe," writes one historian, "gathered as much information for antisemitic purposes with such autonomy of aims and methods" as did the French.

Is this my beloved country, where life and death are so visibly, evidently up for grabs? Is that why I'm here in France?

Because it is such a locus of maddening extremes: seduction and betrayal, beauty and ugliness, love and hate? Because it's such a tease?

———

When you come to France as an immigrant, you are expected to master the language and the history, the philosophy of life, the importance of the Revolution and the creation of the Republic. Then you will be French. You are told the Republic is there for you, the state will respect and protect you. It will take care of you. No one will be more important than you in the eyes of the state.

Beginning in the second decade of the twentieth century, immigration in France outstripped immigration to America, where strict quotas were imposed. Take the Metro in Paris and you will see just how varied the population is. National Front racism, however, goes hand in glove with the basic French progressive philosophical premise that if you're French you are French and not Other. "Others" in French revolutionary philosophy cannot exist in France.

Here is how one French historian puts it, "The myth of origin that was built upon the events of the Revolution made it impossible for 'foreigners' to have a place in the collective memory of the nation. While many American textbooks celebrate the contributions to the American republic of the various communities that settled in the US over the years, in France immigration is always approached as a question extrinsic to the country's history." This is not out of disdain, but rather out of a passion for universality and equality. To the

French, who believe in the universality the French Republic offers, you are one of them.

This is exactly what makes the French and France so complicated. They do sincerely believe in humanism as the basis for social and political life, but in so doing they disregard *your* particular history, and if you carry that history into your public life, they either ignore it or loathe it. You're either like them or you're nothing. They take you in, but they turn a blind eye to who you are—how you see yourself—in your totality. If immigrants visibly hold on to their origins, they end up living outside the French Republic in ghettos on the outskirts of the city. They are unemployed and despised. They are doomed. The French won't even admit they're there. Just like the way they have begun to teach colonialism in the schools. There is no discussion of why exactly the French went to Mali, Algeria, Morocco, Senegal in the first place. Even if you're middle class and don't suffer the degradations of poverty, you must hide your past life, its marvels and conundrums. Both sides lose in this arrangement, in more or less violent psychological and social ways.

———

Most French people today are confused about what constitutes a French person, and what is the nature of a French state. Can it be a multicultural society and not be ghettoized? Can they talk about "difference" and not "multiculturalism?" They are terrified of becoming a war-torn, permanently divided country like South Africa used to be and Lebanon is today. Do they have to have quotas? An idea they despise. The questions are almost as intense as they are in Israel. Do all

Israelis have to be Jewish? Does it have to be a Jewish state? What about Palestinian Israelis? Le Pen would say "Citizens have equal rights, not men." He does not think that African immigrants are citizens.

Often, the same people who wonder openly, Whither their country, are the ones whose knee-jerk pride in being French precludes their listening to any criticism. You talk about the Collaboration, they talk about the coercion of the Germans. You mention the anger of European French in the streets today, they haven't noticed. You say, You know, art and literature are dead here. They shrug their shoulders. They endlessly complain about how hard they are working, and they are constantly going on vacation. Few of them seem driven by much of anything. But then one of them opens a small business and is recruiting employees. She finds the passivity of the chronically unemployed annoying. Why can't the French be more like the English, she wonders. She also notices that the bureaucrats never really tried to find her a job when she was unemployed, and what parasites they are, living off the state. People who work for the state, perhaps, shouldn't have their jobs for life, she muses.

The French pick away here and there at economic interpretations and answers, but they never talk about what's wrong with who they are and what they have actually become. Even the most enlightened among them will bring their Jewish friends Christmas presents on Hanukkah or put up a Christmas tree for their little boy and insist they are not Christian. They are incapable of admitting their blind spots. Probably because they know if they do, the whole edifice will crumble.

I go to visit Muriel in the hospital after she's given birth, and when I call to tell her I'm stopping by, she tells me that another friend will be there too. While we're on the phone, she tells me a little bit about this person. When I arrive, I find that her friend is black. In the United States, in such a situation, my friend would have told me that the other person was black. It never entered Muriel's mind. To her, her friend is French. I'm impressed. But now I wonder how easy it is for her friend to find a job.

My friend Brigitte has many Jewish friends in film and theater. By chance, she has also done readings of Jewish medieval and renaissance poetry at the Jewish Museum in Paris. She herself is from an *haute bourgeois* Catholic family. At the end of last summer, she and Ken and I spent a day in Fecamp, on the Normandy coast not far from Etretat, where Monet made his glorious paintings of the cliff. Brigitte has just bought a house there. We have a typical Brigittian day. We start at about 11:30 A.M., having lunch in a restaurant overlooking the beach and Channel. We drink and eat together half the day, until Brigitte suggests, pointing to a café down the boardwalk, that we go there for coffee. We do, and linger in the sun, sheltered under an umbrella, for another couple of hours. Then she takes us to a church she likes that has some lovely sculpture and one figure of a saint whose foot is worn down from being touched, like that onyx green statue of St. Peter's in Rome. She insists that I touch the foot. "It will bring you good luck," she says. I don't want to, but I can't refuse her. All day afterward, I feel guilty and worried. Finally we hike up to a restaurant on the cliff where our hotel is, and we have dinner. It's a lovely day, the best sort of day with a friend, where conversation ranges over family and movies and, in this case, French Jews.

At dinner I express my unhappiness, even anger, with the Jewish Museum in Paris. I find it polite and tasteful, like so much in French culture that seems so lifeless, and cowardly to me. Brigitte says, "It's a museum for a small public, the French Jewish community. They can learn about themselves there." That's all she says. But I remember Muriel once commenting, "It seems like Jews in America are Jews, but in France they're French."

French Jews don't know who they are, because the price of admission to the French Republic is to be French and not Jewish. So if a Jew wants to be French, she must hide her Jewish identity and history in public. She must assimilate so well that she forgets her past and has nothing Jewish embedded in her present that might accidentally escape into public view. This Jew needs the museum to shyly, politely tell her who she is and who she was.

Where is her rage, I wonder? If she and all the other Jews assimilated so well, how did the Germans get them? Or rather, why were the French Milice, the Vichy version of the Gestapo, so eager to get them? They were French, after all, weren't they? Similarly, everyone now pretends that the Algerian French are French, but everyone knows they are not. They are too Algerian to be French.

Facile certainties won't work, though, because Jews like Léon Blum, Mendès France, and Laurent Fabius can become prime ministers in France. Jews are everywhere in public life. They publish, produce films, write sociology, philosophy, and anthropology, make scientific discoveries, contribute to the editorial pages of newspapers. France's treatment of Israel is interesting, too. Israeli politics are almost universally abhorred, but Israeli culture—music, film, literature—is everywhere appreciated, analyzed, celebrated in all its particularities. In the States, Israel seems only to be a question of Israeli versus Palestinian. There is no other discourse; there are no individual Israelis or Palestinians.

So Jews have also thrived in France, in the French Republic. But Algerians have not. Nor have other Africans or Asians.

—

France has murdered, smothered, and restrained her citizens, and she won't admit it. You cannot hide a murder. Edgar Allan Poe, one of France's favorite authors, made this urge and its impossibility his stock in trade. So did Freud. Maybe the image of Medea is apt for France. The loving Mother— Mary in her soft folded fabrics, or Marianne in her rougher ones—killing her own children. "Vichy was not only the end of the process of Jewish emancipation begun by the Revolution," writes one historian, "it was also the brutal destruction of Franco-Judaism." If French Jews survived the camps and returned to France, they frequently didn't tell their children what had happened, or even sometimes that they were Jewish. They blamed it on the Germans, one of the many reasons France has taken so very long to look honestly at Vichy. The Jews wanted to be French, not Jewish. Even *after* the Holocaust.

To this day, the war in Algeria is ignored. The French won't talk openly about it. It is all of a piece. If they looked at the Algerian war, they would have to look at Vichy. They won't do it. What the French need to do is what South Africans did after the end of apartheid. They need a Truth and Reconciliation Commission, imperfect as it was. The French are incapable of admitting their errors, though, either as public citizens or as private individuals. Who can imagine them day after day listening to Algerians and Jews accusing them of murder and torture? And then apologizing.

A shopkeeper will not apologize if he gives you the wrong change. The woman at the laundry will reply to your complaints that she's been returning your sheets with holes in them with, "No one else tells me that." De Gaulle after the war said that Pétain had been a great soldier, the victor at Verdun and the savior of France during World War I. De Gaulle denied that Pétain had presided over the destruction of the Republic. Who can imagine proud France washing her dirty laundry in public?

Is there a relationship between the French not admitting their faults, and their deep distaste for Others, who they undoubtedly see as "making mistakes," being imperfect, all the time? A recent cruelty at an Air France departure desk brings this point home: A man is trying to board an Air France flight in Delhi to Paris. He is stopped at the desk and told he has to buy an extra ticket because of his size. He is not only told this, but he is weighed and measured in full view of other passengers. This man is obese, and to be treated in such a humiliating way seems right at home in France and not elsewhere. He is bringing charges of discrimination against Air France, but to date nothing has happened. Since France is a far less us culture than ours is, and a slimmer one, and a more judgmental one when it comes to those who vary from their norm—those who are Others—I wager that this man will receive no recompense. Air France will not admit its error. It will not apologize.

—

I think this is what happened to France. She suffered a traumatic injury in World War I. Her body—her soul—was near mortally wounded. She tended the wound, but only superficially. Then she wrapped herself securely in the past. She appended this war to her national story, and there it hardened, like the Republic and its credo itself, into a fetish. The pain and rage are still alive in the fetish. Tenderly the French turned, in the 1920s, to their sweet earth, as to the hem of Mary, and on it they wept for their land. When any untoward ripple or mishap arrived, they called it "foreign," German, "Other"—and they deplored it with a rage and self-righteousness that only repressed emotions can produce.

World War II remains a splinter they can't pull out. First they lie about it, then they glorify the little they did that was good, and they blame the rest on the Germans. When Marcel Ophuls's film *The Sorrow and the Pity* arrived in 1971 and exposed the ugly extent of their collaboration, they banned it. It was a distortion, absolutely *not* the truth about them. This denial has become ignorance in their young.

The French must take responsibility for their blindness and their cowardice, in the Twenties, in Vichy, and in Algeria. The French are sick in their soul, and that is why their culture is dying. Their lying history is strangling them to death. They smooth everything over with their good taste. At all costs they sidestep conflict. Everything is neutralized. Nothing takes flight, nothing soars.

The French cannot face the fact that as a nation they have not put into practice their highest values, they have not offered liberty, fraternity, equality to all their citizens. They cannot admit this because if they do, who are they then? Certainly not the great French nation. Of course they are worrying about disappearing: They have practically disappeared already.

I have a modest suggestion to make, based on the writings of recent French philosophers and historians. It's a homework assignment, to be done in the evenings when the French are resting from the Truth and Reconciliation Commission hearings. They should begin to think about their own multiple identities, the differences among the French of European roots. They might be less frightened and disdainful of others if they did that. France is made up of many regions, each with its own profile. Towns are made up of many people. Some of these collaborated, some resisted, some waited. Some are Catholics, some Protestants; there are atheists, Muslims, Jews, Freemasons. Most don't give a damn one way or the other. Joan of Arc means something different to each of them. So do the tricolor, the Marseillaise, the Republic. Unities are false; they are mirages. If the French really saw their own multifacetedness, they would let Others in, because they would see the Other in themselves.

Perhaps it might be possible even to understand their revolution in these terms. The Third Estate, that growing middle class, as well as the Fourth Estate of workers, peasants, and unemployed, were Other to the aristocrats, the court, and the Church. Later on, workers became Other to the middle classes. These conflicts have always ended in large or small revolutions. But the "Others" entered France one way or another. And France has soared with them. They must know that. Which direction will French flight take in the future?

—

When I was working on the book about my father and his brother, and my father was very old, we talked about his childhood. He remembered things he hadn't before. Like most people's, his stories were a patchwork of repeated phrases. Like the French and their story of their history. But one day he told me something new. He remembered what happened to him on a street in Riga when he was six years old.

German soldiers were quartered in the town, and there was an outbreak of violence in my father's neighborhood. His mother wanted him to do something for her. He was small and fast. She bundled him up against the cold and filled his pockets with cigarettes and soap and sugar.

"You understand, *mein kind*," Grandma said, adjusting his little jacket. "You go up to the soldiers and smile and ask them if they'd like to buy some tobacco or soap. Always get the money before you give them anything. That's not hard, *kindela*, is it?"

"No, Mama." She took his head in her hands, kissed him on the mouth, and pushed him into the street.

People were running. There was smoke and noise everywhere. Little Louis, my father, headed toward an arcade to hide, but instead he slammed into the leg of a German soldier, who lifted him high above his head and, laughing in his face, said, "And what have we got here? Look here, Gerd," he said to another soldier. "Look at this Jewish little boy. You're Jewish, little boy, aren't you?" "Yes," the little boy noded. "And have you got something that we want, little boy?" "Y-yes, Sir, I do," he stammered. He wet himself.

"Anything else, Dad?" I ask.

"No."

"Sure?"

He waved his hand at me, his face twisted up.

How did the soldiers know he was Jewish? It must have been the way they always know.

My grandma did this to him, and he never forgave her, but he never stopped longing for her, either. He got all screwed up, my pop. It ruined him. He flitted from person to person, whoever was handy, whoever would pay attention. He was charming and heartless, and took no one in. He betrayed his own brother.

Maybe he was in some sort of contest with Dave about who was the real man. Dave was said to be effeminate. He never had a girlfriend. Yet he became the soldier and went to Spain. What about Louis? The boxer, the handball player, the guy who drove to Miami on a whim because he felt like watching a jai-alai game or wanted to take a boat to Havana. What about him? Wasn't he a man? Maybe he was still remembering his mother all those years ago on the day she abandoned him and on the day he disappointed her.

He didn't know much, my Pop. He didn't have much self-knowledge. What he had was longing, longing enough to break your heart.

France has lost its most powerful model and not found another. Despite the chilling forecast, I stay. Sensual pleasures thicken my experience of daily life, exhilirating me mentally and emotionally. The rich French social fabric that provides humane and universal health care and financial security, a population that loves to get to know someone else through conversation, all this satisfies me. It makes me hopeful about what people can be to one another. Perhaps generous impulses can prevail over savage ones. I'm hoping France can change.

I know now why I came here. I wanted to forgive my father. He gave me dreams and literature. He made me hunger for a man's body. I learned desire from him, even if he couldn't really love me. I know that fear eats the soul and love pushes the horizon to infinity. That's what I've learned living in France. It's why I stay.

Endnotes

INTRODUCTION

14.   "I am sitting on": Letter from Dave Lipton to his parents from Spain, July 10, 1938. In the author's possession.

1. MOTHER

28.   "One day in winter": Marcel Proust, *In Search of Lost Time*, formerly titled *Remembrance of Things Past* (the translation the author used), transl. C. K. Scott Moncrieff and Terence Kilmartin (New York, 1982; orig. 1913), Vol. 1, p. 48.

38.   "We need food": Letter from Dave Lipton to his parents, July 10, 1938.

41.   "The feeling of satisfaction": Cited in Benedetta Craveri, *The Age of Conversation*, transl. Teresa Waugh (New York, 2005), p. 372.

44.   "tall girl . . . emerge": Proust, *Remembrance of Things Past,* (original edition, 1919), pp. 705–706.

50.   "No, no, leave": Ibid., p. 29.

50.   "I was stirred": Ibid., p. 30.

50.	"Then, suddenly . . . my anxiety subsided": Ibid., p. 34.
52.	"You ask me": Colette, *Break of Day*, transl. Enid McLeod (New York, 1961; orig. 1928), pp. 1–2. In Judith Thurman's biography of Colette, Thurman points out that the original letter was quite different from the one Colette published in her book. See Thurman's *Secrets of the Flesh: A Life of Colette* (New York, 1999), p. 234.
62.	*"The Outsider"*: Albert Camus, *The Outsider*, transl. Joseph Laredo (London, 2000; formerly translated as *The Stranger*; orig. 1942).
62.	"he'd been surprised": Ibid., p. 86.
63.	"He answered the questions": Ibid., p. 87.
63.	"is he being accused": Ibid., p. 93.

2. TEASE

68.	"Like all my books": Some of the material in this section appeared in different form in the author's "Women, Pleasure and Painting (e.g., Boucher)," *Genders* 7 (Spring 1990): pp. 69–86.
69.	"One acerbic colleague": Carol Duncan, "Fallen Fathers: Images of Authority in Pre-Revolutionary French Art," *Art History* 4 (June 1981), pp. 186–202; "When Greatness is a Box of Wheaties," *Artforum* 63 (Oct. 1975), pp. 60–64.

ENDNOTES

74. "I once read": Jane Gallop, *The Daughter's Seduction: Feminism and Psychoanalysis* (New York, 1982), pp. 30–31.

74. "Another critic wrote": Julia Kristeva, "About Chinese Women," in *The Kristeva Reader*, ed. Toril Moi (New York, 1986), p. 142.

78. "We fashioned games": Lenet is describing what he witnessed at Chantilly in the mid-seventeenth century. Quoted in Thomas E. Crow, *Painters and Public Life in Eighteenth-Century Paris* (New Haven and London, 1985), p. 68.

78–79. "He never chanced": Cited in Craveri, *The Age of Conversation*, p. 247.

80. "Louis XIV 'loved'": Jacques Revel, "The Court," in Pierre Nora, *Realms of Memory: Rethinking the French Past*, Vol. II, transl. Arthur Goldhammer (New York, 1996), p. 77.

81. "Boucher earned": Crow, *Painters and Public Life in Eighteenth-Century Paris*, p. 11.

82. "Born Jeanne-Antoinette Poisson": Voltaire, *Memoires pour Servir à la Vie* (Paris, 1998), p. 105. Cited in Christine Pevitt Algrant, *Madame de Pompadour: Mistress of France* (New York, 2002), p. 23.

84. "One in particular": This portrait was painted in 1756 and is located today in the Alte Pinakothek, Munich.

86.   "she looked me up": Cited in Elise Goodman, *The Portraits of Madame de Pompadour: Celebrating the Femme Savante* (Berkeley, 2000), pp. 11–20, 10.

86.   "The political philosopher": Cited in Elise Goodman, *The Portraits of Madame de Pompadour: Celebrating the Femme Savante* (Berkeley, 2000), p. 10.

87.   "Voltaire wrote in a letter": Colin Jones, *Madame de Pompadour: Images of a Mistress* (London, 2002), p. 65.

87.   "A small bourgeoise": Evelyne Lever, *Madame de Pompadour: A Life*, transl. Catherine Temerson (New York, 2002), pp. 117, 122.

87.   "More recent writing": Ibid., pp. 91, 121, 260.

88.   "launched a charm offensive": Colin Jones, *Madame de Pompadour: Images of a Mistress*, pp. 47, 88.

88.   "Only a few feminist historians": See Elise Goodman, *Portraits of Madame de Pompadour*, and also the work of Ewa Lajer-Burcharth, Melissa Hyde, and Erica Rand.

88.   "that anguished feeling": Craveri, *Age of Conversation*, p. 254.

89.   "I've seen so many": Lever, *Madame de Pompadour*, p. 126, 128, 127.

90.   "As one writer put it": Craveri, *Age of Conversation*, p. 299.

91.   "Montesquieu, as early as 1721": Charles-Louis
        de Secondat, Baron de Montesquieu, *Persian Let-
        ters*, transl. C. J. Betts (Harmondsworth, 1973),
        p. 197.

92.   "How could you have": Ibid., p. 280.

92.   "too many women fall: Denis Diderot, "On
        Women," in *Dialogues*, transl. F. Birrell
        (London, 1927), pp. 195–196.

92.   "Woman has inside her": Ibid., p. 190.

92.   "artificial sentiment which": Quoted in Linda
        Zerilli, "Motionless Idols and Virtuous Mothers:
        Women, Art and Politics in France, 1789–1848,"
        Berkeley Journal of Sociology 27 (1982): 93.

92.   "Whatever she may do": Quoted in Joan Landes,
        *Women and the Public Sphere in the Age of the
        French Revolution* (Ithaca, 1988), p. 85.

93.   "be honest and hard working": Quoted in
        Margaret H. Darrow, "French Noblewomen and
        the New Domesticity," *Feminist Studies* 5 (1979):
        64.

93.   "Be a woman": Cited in Landes, *Women and the
        Public Sphere*, p. 145.

93   "I have entirely devoted": Ibid., p. 167

94.   "A husband owes protection": George Rudé,
        Revolutionary Europe, 1783–1815 (New York,
        1975), p. 233.

94.   "What we ask of education": Ibid., p. 235.

94.   "Mme Geoffrin did not even participate": Craveri,
       Age of Conversation, passim, pp. 298–302, 301.

94.   "Lespinasse, at the beginning": Judith Curtis, *"The
       Epistolières,"* French Women and the Age of
       Enlightenment, ed. Samia I. Spencer
       (Bloomington, 1984), pp. 228, 234.

95.   "The power of women": Steven Kale, *French
       Salons: High Society and Political Sociability from
       the Old Regime to the Revolution of 1848*
       (Baltimore, 2004), pp. 40–41.

97.   "Luxury is an extremely": Colin Jones, *The Great
       Nation: France from Louis XV to Napoleon*
       (New York, 2002), p. 190.

97.   "The *Encyclopédie* informs us ": Cited in Ibid., p. 191.

99.   "not only the satisfactions": I owe my friend and
       editor Jean Casella far, far more than a footnote.

3. THAT SUNSHINE

104.   "That is what the French philosopher":
       Emmanuel Levinas, *Difficult Freedom: Essays in
       Judaism*, transl. Seán Hand (Baltimore, 1990;
       orig. 1963 and 1976). See especially "Ethics and
       Spirit," pp. 6–8.

107.   "Charming style": Rachel Cohen, *A Chance
       Meeting: Intertwined Lives of American Writers and
       Artists, 1854–1967* (New York, 2004), p. 37.

108.   "When I look at Monet's": *The Magpie* was
         painted in 1869 and is located at the Musée
         d'Orsay, Paris.

109.   *"Dance at the Moulin de la Galette"*: painted in
         1876, located at the Musée d'Orsay, Paris.

111.   "Does it matter": Jean Renoir, *Renoir, My Father*,
         transl. Randolph and Dorothy Weaver
         (Boston, 1958), pp. 88, 361.

111.   "John Berger, the English critic": John Berger,
         Ways of Seeing (Harmondsworth, 1972),
         pp. 27–28.

113.   "I felt then that": Louisine Havemeyer, *Sixteen to
         Sixty: Memoirs of a Collector*, ed. Susan A. Stein
         (New York, 1993), pp. 269–270.

117.   "It is remarkable": Meyer Schapiro, "The Nature
         of Abstract Art," in *Modern Art, 19th & 20th
         Centuries: Selected Papers* (New York, 1978; orig.
         1937), p. 192.

118.   "It is, it seems, the destiny": Prominent leftist
         critics of Impressionism are Linda Nochlin,
         T. J. Clark, and Robert Herbert.

118.   "all great works of art": Walter Benjamin, *Theses
         on the Philosophy of History*, 1939–1940), cited in
         John Berger, *John Berger: Selected Essays*, ed.
         Geoff Dyer (London, 2001), p. 190.

119.   "Jewish intellectuals like": For a discussion of
         Jews in art history, see the author's "The Hill

Behind the House: An Ashkenazi Jew and Art History," in *Diaspora and Visual Culture: Representing Africans and Jews*, ed. Nicholas Mirzoeff (New York, 2000), pp.179–189; and the same subject at greater length, "The Pastry Shop and the Angel of Death: What's Jewish in Art History,"in *People of the Book: Thirty Scholars Reflect on their Jewish Identity*, eds. Shelley Fisher Fishkin and Jeffrey Rubin-Dorsky (Madison, 1996), pp. 280–97.

121. "They were everywhere": The discussion of Degas's laundresses in this chapter appeared in another form in the author's *Looking into Degas: Uneasy Images of Women and Modern Life*, Ch. 3: "Images of Laundresses: Social and Sexual Ambivalence" (Berkeley, 1986), pp. 116–150.

121. "Zola writes in his novel": Emile Zola, *L'Assommoir*, transl. Leonard Tancock, (Harmondsworth, 1970; orig. 1876), pp. 143, 191.

126. "Our Paris, the Paris": Jules and Edmond de Goncourt, cited in T. J. Clark, *The Painting of Modern Life: Paris in the Art of Manet and his Follower* (Princeton, 1999), p. 34.

126. "The crowd is his": Charles Baudelaire, "The Painter of Modern Life," *Selected Writings on Art and Artists*, transl. P. E. Charvet (Harmondsworth, 1972; orig. 1863), p. 399.

127.   "A tart? No": Emile Zola, *Ladies' Delight*, transl. April Fitzlyon (London, 1958; orig. 1882), p. 97.

127.   "did not come [to the café]": Nancy Mowll Mathews, *Mary Cassatt: A Life* (New York, 1994), p. 123.

128.   "Manet's most daring": See the author's *Alias Olympia: A Woman's Search for Manet's Notorious Model and Her Own Desire* (New York, 1992).

129.   "One historian suggests": Robert Herbert, *Art, Leisure, and Parisian Society* (New Haven, 1988), pp. 136–137.

133.   "Degas's one official-looking": This picture was painted between 1880 and 1884 and hangs in the National Portrait Gallery, Smithsonian Institution, Washington D.C.

134.   "He sent her several letters": Edgar Germain Hilaire Degas, *Letters*, ed. Marcel Guérin, transl. Marguerite Kay (Oxford, 1947), pp. 199, 203, 204.

135.   "So, he has died": Ralph Shikes and Paula Harper, *Pissarro: His Life and Work* (New York, 1980), p. 308.

135.   "symbol of their": Pierre Birnbaum, "Grégoire, Dreyfus, Drancy, and the Rue Copernic: Jews at the Heart of French History," in Pierre Nora, *Realms of Memory: Rethinking the French Past*, Vol. I, transl. Arthur Goldhammer (New York, 1996), p. 406.

136.   "what settled the fate": Alfred Cobban, *A History of Modern France: Vol. 3: 1871–1962* (Harmondsworth, 1965), p. 49.

136.   "The affair will be hushed": Paula E. Hyman, *The Jews of Modern France* (Berkeley, 1998), p. 101.

137.   "had given the anti-Semites": Cobban, *A History*, Vol. 3, p. 50.

137.   "Did Degas think": Linda Nochlin, "Degas and the Dreyfus Affair: A Portrait of the Artist as an Anti-Semite," *The Politics of Vision: Essays on Nineteenth-Century Art and Society* (New York, 1989), p. 156.

137.   "In an article of 1898 . . . Pissarro sent a copy": Cited in Shikes and Harper, *Pissarro*, p. 307.

138.   "Jews shouldn't be allowed": Barbara Ehrlich White, *Renoir, His Life, Art, and Letters* (New York, 1984), pp. 121, 210–211; cited in Nochlin, "Degas and the Dreyfus Affair," *Politics of Vision*, p. 142.

138.   "My duty is to speak": "The Law Report," Radio National of Australia: http://www.abc.net.au/rn/talks/8.30/lawrpt/stories/s1612922.htm; "I accuse": Hyman, *Jews of Modern France*, pp. 104–105.

138.   "A lowly priest": Quoted in Birnbaum, "Grégoire, Dreyfus, Drancy," p. 407.

139.   "In Degas's painting *At*": This work was painted in 1878–1879 and is located at the Louvre.

4. WHAT GLORY

142.   "Not nearly as enchanting": Edmonde Charles-Roux, *The World of Coco Chanel: Friends, Fashion, Fame* (London, 2005; orig. 1981), p. 274.

142.   "'Amateur' was no longer": Thanks to Whitney Chadwick's and Tirza True Latimer's edited collection of essays *The Modern Woman Revisited: Paris Between the Wars* (New Brunswick, 2003), we now have an extensive new view of the Modern Woman that includes issues of race and sexual choice.

144.   "One teachers' organization": Cited in Theodore Zeldin, *France 1848–1945*, vol. two: *Intellect, Taste and Anxiety* (Oxford, 1977), p. 665.

145.   "She made her entry": Janet Flanner, *Paris Was Yesterday: 1925–1939* (New York, 1972), p. xx.

145.   "The cream of the Negro musicians": Tyler Stovall, *Paris Noir: African Americans in the City of Light* (Boston, 1996), pp. 58–59.

146.   "Canute Frankson, a": http://www.albavalb.org/curriculum/index.php?module=8&page=P010; then hit "Canute Frankson" and Cary Nelson and Jefferson Hendricks, eds., *Madrid 1937: Letters of the Abraham Lincoln Brigade from the Spanish Civil War* (New York, 1996).

147.   "The idea that a black man": Tyler Stovall, "Gender, Race, and Miscegenation: African

Americans in Jazz Age Paris," in Chadwick and Latimer's *The Modern Woman Revisited*, p. 28.

147.   "Soon after the war": Cited in Stovall, *Paris Noir*, p. 27.

147.   "Ten of these were": Stovall, *Paris Noir*, p. 27.

147.   "France was deep": See Wanda Corn's lively treatment of the French love affair with things American in her *The Great American Thing: Modern Art and National Identity, 1915–1935* (Berkeley, 2000), especially Ch. 2, "An American in Paris," pp. 91–133.

148.   "I was urged by my friends": Elliot Paul, *The Last Time I Saw Paris* (London, 2001; orig. 1942), p. 96.

148.   "cassia, cloves, caraway": Paul, *The Last Time I Saw Paris*, p. 62.

149.   "Here's a description": Dada started during World War I in Zurich among a small group of international artists, writers, and composers like Tristan Tzara, the Romanian poet; Hugo Ball, a German writer and musician; Richard Huelsenbeck, a poet and medical student; Jean (Hans) Arp, an artist, born in Alsace with German nationality; and Hans Richter, a German artist and filmmaker. It continued in Paris and in New York with the great addition of Marcel Duchamp. They were a vehemently non-object-making group of artists. The

ENDNOTES

	Tzara quote is cited in Malcolm Cowley, *Exile's Return* (New York, 1951), pp. 138–139.
149.	"for the first time": Cowley, *Exile's Return*, p. 139.
152.	"I am seeking the France": Benjamin Stora, *Algeria, 1830–2000: A Short History*, transl. Jane Marie Todd; Forward, William B. Quandt (Ithaca, 2001), pp. 17, 66.
152.	"I was forced to admit": James Baldwin, *Notes of a Native Son* (Boston, 1955), pp. 7, 9.
155.	"My father knew": Sarah Kofman, *Rue Ordener, Rue Labat*, transl. Ann Smock (Lincoln, 1996), pp. 5–6, 9.
157.	"Before the armistice": Antoine Prost, "Monuments to the Dead," *Realms of Memory: Rethinking the French Past*, vol. 2, ed. Pierre Nora, transl. Arthur Goldhammer (New York, 1997), p. 309.
159.	*"The Ghost Road"*: *Regeneration* (1991), *The Eye in the Door* (1993), *The Ghost Road* (1995), all published originally by Viking Press, London.
159.	"lost in dead": Cobban, *A History: Vol. 3*, p. 111.
159.	"The Germans had massed": Antoine Prost, "Verdun," *Realms of Memory: Rethinking the French Past*, vol. 3, ed. Pierre Nora, transl. Arthur Goldhammer (New York, 1998), pp. 396, 397.
160.	"They were like convicts": Georges Gaudy, *Les Trous d'obus de Verdun* [The Shell Craters of

Verdun] (Paris, 1922) cited in Prost, "Verdun,"
Realms of Memory, p. 398.

160.   "The thing I used to notice": Amanda Vaill, *Everybody Was So Young: Gerald and Sara Murphy: A
Lost Generation Love Story* (Boston, 1998), p. 99.

160.   "Let it be over": Simone de Beauvoir, *Memoirs of a
Dutiful Daughter*, transl. James Kirkup
(New York, 1974; orig. 1958), p. 65.

160.   "In Hemingway's *A Farewell*": Ernest Hemingway,
A Farewell to Arms (London, 2004; orig. 1929),
pp. 159–161.

162.   "I . . . saw the quality": Ernest Hemingway, *A
Moveable Feast* (London, 2004; orig. 1964), p. 47.

162.   "[She] is quietly": Elliot Paul, *Last Time I Saw
Paris*, p. 63.

165.   "They were also shimmering": see Alfred Cobban,
A History, Vol. 3, p. 61.

165.   "In 1919 for the first time": Ibid., p. 123.

166.   "Throughout the decade": Quoted in Mary Louise
Roberts, "Samson and Delilah Revisited: The Poli-
tics of Fashion in 1920s France," in Chadwick and
Latimer, eds., *The Modern Woman Revisited*, p. 65.

166–67.   "most immediate, and most influential": Kenneth E.
Silver, *Esprit de Corps: The Art of the Parisian
Avant-Garde and the First World War, 1914–1925*
(London, 1989), p. 283.

168.   "acquired an astonishing": Cobban, *A History: Vol. 3*, p. 132.

168.   "The intolerance that conservative": Romy Golan brilliantly and daringly develops this theme in *Modernity and Nostalgia: Art and Politics in France between the Wars* (New Haven, 1995). It will be obvious how deeply indebted I am to this inspiring and groundbreaking work; the latter part of this chapter is fundamentally shaped by her insights.

169.   "I am delighted with what": Silver, *Esprit de Corps*, p. 147.

169.   "Is There Such a Thing": Golan, *Modernity and Nostalgia*, pp. 138–139.

169.   "Here come the holidays": Golan, *Modernity and Nostalgia*, p. 88.

169.   "It isn't a question": All quoted in Golan, *Modernity and Nostalgia*, pp. 140, 142.

170.   "Does one detect": Romy Golan, "From Fin de Siècle to Vichy: The Cultural Hygienics of Camille (Faust) Mauclair," Linda Nochlin and Tamar Garb, eds., *The Jew in the Text: Modernity and the Construction of Identity* (London, 1995), pp. 168, 169–170.

170.   "But it was the writer": Golan writes at length about Mauclair in *Modernity and Nostalgia*, but also devotes an entire article to him, "From Fin de

Siècle to Vichy," in Nochlin and Garb, eds., *The Jew in the Text*, pp. 156–173, 317–320.

170. "Montparnasse, inhabited as": Golan, *Modernity and Nostalgia*, p. 151.

171. "A kind of benign classicism": See Silver, *Esprit de Corps*, passim.

171. "the *paysan* was god": *"Paysan"* does not translate into English as "peasant." It is more like "person of the land" or "of the country-side."

171. "In the darkest hours": Quoted in Golan, *Modernity and Nostalgia*, p. 40.

172. "Utrillo's work depicts": André Chamson, "Les Oeuvres récentes d'Utrillo," *Formes*, June 1930, cited in Golan, *Modernity and Nostalgia*, p. 49.

173. "Better Hitler than [the Jew and socialist]": In fact there was no such title, Prime Minister, until after World War II. At the time, people would have referring to President of the Council.

174. "Our France which bleeds": Cited in Silver, *Esprit de Corps*, pp. 7–8.

5. FLIGHT

178. "the first time as tragedy": Karl Marx, *The Eighteenth Brumaire of Louis Bonaparte* (New York, 1975; orig. 1852), p. 15.

190. *"Le Monde* asked an": Olivier Poivre d'Arvor, "Les

artistes français contemporains s'exportent badly,"
[French artists export badly], *Le Monde*, June 11, 2005.

194.   "One day we will find": John Golding, "The
Triumph of Picasso," *The New York Review of
Books* 35 (July 21, 1988): file:///Users/eunicelipton/
Documents/I%20LOVE%20YOU,%20NOT%20RE
ALLY:Le%20Baby/—CODA%20%20France%20
Run%20Amok/Bks%20&%20%22articles%22/John
%20Golding,%20NYRB,%20Demoiselles,%20etc.
webarchive, p. 2.

194.   "It has become clear": Vivian Gornick has written
formidably about this subject in *The End of the
Novel of Love* (Boston, 1997).

196.   "That mysterious 'other'": Benjamin Stora, *Algeria*,
p. 93.

196.   "that to be a Negro": James Baldwin, *Notes of a
Native Son* (Boston, 1955), p. 93, 94.

196.   "mutilated by oppression": James D. Le Sueur,
*Uncivil War: Intellectuals and Identity Politics
During the Decolonization of Algeria*
(Philadelphia, 2001), p. 221.

197.   "Leftists refused to admit": Le Sueur, *Uncivil War*,
p. 244.

198.   "France abandoned its children": Marco Werman
interview of Monsieur R, PRI (Public Radio
International) broadcast, March 13, 2006.

199.   "the readiness of state commissions": Rod
Kedward, *La Vie en Bleu: France and the French
Since 1900* (London, 2005), p. 560.

199.   "My friend, do you know": Cited in Julian
Jackson, *France: The Dark Years 1940–1944*
(Oxford, 2001), p. 279.

200.   "periodic eczema". . . "While the war
[World War I]": Ibid., pp. 40, 41.

200.   "Today, National Front": See Anti-Defamation
League site: http://www.adl.org/international/
LePen-2-history.asp.

200.   "First, officials blamed": Marco Werman interview
of Monsieur R; PRI (Public Radio International)
broadcast, March 13, 2006.

202.   "On 16 and 17 July": Kedward, *La Vie en Bleu*,
p. 265–266.

202.   "No other authority": Ibid., p. 264.

203.   "The myth of origin": Gérard Noiriel, "French and
Foreigners," in Nora, *Realms of Memory*, Vol. I, p. 151.

208.   "Vichy was not only": Pierre Birnbaum, "Grégoire,
Dreyfus, Drancy," in Nora, *Realms of Memory*,
Vol. I, p. 410.

211.   "I have a modest": One of the most important pub-
lications in this area is Pierre Nora, ed., *Realms of
Memory: Rethinking the French Past*, transl. Arthur
Goldhammer, 3 vols. (New York, 1996–1998).

Acknowledgments

Thanks to Muriel Boselli in Paris, source of endless Franco–English–American revelations. And to Ed Alcock for the author photo he generously made. Stuart Jeffries's wit, generosity, and wide knowledge exhilarated me. Kay Holmes's wildness and intrepid orneriness buoyed my spirit; so did her sharp editorial comments. Chantal Maillet I thank for her dependable correspondence, day or night, and for her patient reading of my text when I most needed an informed and politically engaged French reader. In New York, I thank Keith Wallman at Carroll & Graf for his attentive editing of my manuscript and his kindness and patience with my anxieties. And I am grateful to Jean Casella for her searing questions. I learned more than I can say from her psychological wisdom, political savvy, and word wizardry. I thank Meryl Schwartz for her skepticism and loyalty, and Joan Rosenbaum for her discriminating enthusiams. My indefatigable and cheeky agent, Charlotte Cecil Raymond, never let me down. And my husband, Ken Aptekar, I thank for everything, but especially his patience and humor (in all senses), his great editing skill, and his startling selflessness in urging me into the arms of a gorgeous French thirteenth-century convent-turned-hotel where for two months I worked devoutly and deliriously. And finally to that marvel of places itself, le Couvent Royal in Saint-Maximin-la-Sainte-Baume and the ever-considerate Agnès Brant and Nicolas Desanti, merci!

About the Author

Eunice Lipton divides her time between New York and Paris. She studied history and literature at The City College of New York and received her Ph.D. in art history at NYU's Institute of Fine Arts. She is the author of *Alias Olympia, Looking Into Degas,* and *Picasso Criticism, 1901–1939: The Making of an Artist Hero.* She lives with the artist Ken Aptekar.